"Your father's ruby ring," Sam whispered. "It's gone!"

Wishbone's nails clicked on the steps as he ran up to Wanda's balcony office. He squeezed in between Wanda and Sam, then jumped onto a chair. The glass cube lay on its side, empty.

"I knew I should have taken the ring to the bank sooner," Wanda said. She gazed in shock at the empty cube. "Now it's gone!"

The others crowded around the desk behind Wishbone, all talking at once.

"But how did the thief get in and out?" Sam asked. "The front door was locked. So were the gates over the windows on the fire escape."

"Maybe there's another open window?" Isabel suggested.

Wanda shook her head. "This is the only one I opened."

"Does anyone else have a key?" Kayla asked.

Wanda shook her head again.

Putting his muzzle to the ground, Wishbone began sniffing. "Tracking Dog is on the case.

But . . . where are the clues?"

To Sniff A Thief

A. D. Francis

A Division of Lyrick Publishing™

WISHBONE™
created by Rick Duffield

Big Red Chair Books™, A Division of **Lyrick Publishing**™
300 E. Bethany Drive, Allen, Texas 75002

Produced by By George Productions, Inc.
Interior Illustrations by Steven Petruccio

Library of Congress Catalog Card Number: 99-67696
ISBN: 1-57064-841-7

First printing: July 2000
Printed in the United States of America
10 9 8 7 6 5 4 3 2

Acknowledgements

The author wishes to acknowledge E. W. Hornung for his inspiring work, *The Amateur Cracksman.* The author also thanks Anne Capeci, who understands the dog so well.

Chapter One

"Red alert!" Wishbone wagged his tail and sniffed the Friday afternoon air. "My pizza radar is picking up some strong signals. Garlic, cheese, and . . . is that pepperoni?" The white-with-brown-and-black-spots Jack Russell terrier perked up his ears and looked back over his haunches. "Joe? David? Come on!"

Wishbone's best buddy, fourteen-year-old Joe Talbot, was just walking around the corner onto Oak Street, wearing jeans and his basketball jacket. His dark hair was tousled, and the cold autumn wind had whipped color into his cheeks. Next to Joe was David Barnes, a tall boy with dark hair and chocolate-brown skin. David was one of Joe and Wishbone's best friends. Wishbone knew that both boys loved pizza almost as much as he did. But they were so busy talking that they didn't appear to have heard Wishbone. The terrier ran back and jumped around their feet, barking.

"I'm talking pizza, guys! Hellllooo!"

"Hey, Wishbone." Joe bent to scratch Wishbone behind his ears, then straightened up and turned back to David. "Did you hear about Sam's baby-sitting job?" he asked.

Samantha Kepler was Joe and Wishbone's other good friend. Her father owned Pepper Pete's Pizza Parlor, where Wishbone, Joe, and David were headed at that very moment. Sam often helped out in the restaurant after school—which didn't leave much time for baby-sitting.

"Baby-sitting?" David asked. "How did Sam get roped into that?"

"Jimmy Kidd's mom is out of town for a few days, and someone has to keep an eye on Jimmy until Mr. Kidd gets home from work tonight. Damont backed out at the last minute because of some project. So Mr. Kidd asked Sam instead."

"And Sam couldn't say no," David finished. "You know Sam."

Wishbone barked his agreement. Sam was one of the most responsible, loyal people a dog could have the pleasure of knowing. "That's Sam, all right! She's always—"

"Joe! David!" a familiar voice called out from behind them.

Wishbone wagged his tail when he caught sight of Sam riding toward them on her bike. Her long blond hair flew out behind her. She wore jeans and a heavy sweater that matched the blue of her eyes. Today those eyes were filled with concern.

"Have you guys seen Jimmy?" Sam asked as she braked her bike next to Joe, David, and Wishbone.

Both Joe and David shook their heads. "We thought you were baby-sitting him," David said.

"I would be if I could find him." Sam got off her bike and glanced up and down Oak Street. "He was supposed to wait for me outside school. But he didn't."

Wishbone knew eleven-year-old Jimmy Kidd fairly well. Jimmy often played in the park with his Chihuahua, Dinky. Wishbone had romped with them enough to know that Jimmy wasn't the easiest kid to look after. He had a way of getting into trouble—just like his cousin, Damont Jones.

"Never fear, Sam. Tracking Dog is here!" Wishbone's alert brown eyes scanned Oak Street. He spotted kids going into the old brick firehouse that had been converted into Oakdale Sports & Games. People hustled in and out of Beck's Grocery, Rosie's Rendezvous Books and Gifts, the post office, and other businesses along the street. Jimmy wasn't among them.

"I'll help you find him." Wishbone barked his offer, then sniffed the pizza-scented air again. "Of course, I'd rather be tracking down a pepperoni pizza. . . ."

Sam started down Oak Street with her friends. She paused to look through the windows of Oakdale Sports & Games. "Why did I think this would be easy?" she said. "I should have known taking care of Jimmy would be a tough assignment." She moved ahead to Rosie's Rendezvous Books and looked through the doorway for Jimmy.

"We'll help look for him," Joe offered.

David nodded. "The three of us can find him."

"Make that four. Don't forget about the dog!" Wishbone caught sight of a tiny dog up ahead. "Hey, guys! It looks like we're on the right trail. There's Dinky!"

Kicking up his hind paws, Wishbone ran toward Pepper Pete's Pizza Parlor. Dinky was standing outside the entrance with his tiny nose pressed against the glass door. When he saw Wishbone, the little dog let out a series of excited barks.

"Hi, Dinky! It's good to see you, too," Wishbone said, touching noses with the Chihuahua.

"There's Jimmy's dog," Wishbone heard Joe say.

"Jimmy must be inside," David added.

"I knew following the pizza trail was the way to go!" Wishbone cheered.

As soon as Sam pulled open the door to Pepper Pete's, Wishbone and Dinky trotted inside. Their claws clicked on the tiled floor as they hurried over to two tables that had been pushed together in the middle of the pizzeria. Six people sat around the tables. Dinky jumped up and pawed the leg of a brown-haired boy Wishbone recognized right away.

"Aha! It's Jimmy, all right. Tracking Dog always gets his man. But what's this?" Wishbone sniffed the air—and went stiff from whiskers to tail. His super-sensitive nose had picked up . . . "A cat? In Pepper Pete's?"

Wishbone sensed that the cat was nearby. He circled the two tables, smelling the feet of each person he passed.

"There's Damont." Wishbone gazed up at the sharp face and short, dark hair of Jimmy's fourteen-year-old cousin. Damont was a freshman at Wilson High, just like Joe, Sam, and David. Wishbone had seen for himself how competitive Damont could be. He and Joe had been rivals ever since Wishbone was a pup.

"Hi, Isabel!" Wishbone gave a big smile to Isabel

St. Clair, the fourteen-year-old girl sitting next to Damont. She had brown eyes and wavy black hair that fell to her shoulders. Of course, Wishbone was better friends with Isabel's two Dobermans, Iggy and Axel. But they didn't seem to be at Pepper Pete's today.

Wishbone turned to Isabel's parents, who were also sitting at the table. "Hello, Mr. and Mrs. St. Clair. Where are Iggy and Axel?"

Wishbone knew the St. Clairs' dogs would help track down the feline scent in the air. Yet Isabel's family didn't seem to have heard Wishbone's question.

"Excuse me? Hey, everyone, there's a cat in here! Am I the only one who's noticed?" Wishbone let out a bark, but it was no use. Everyone seemed to be busy listening to someone at the end of the table. It was a young woman Wishbone had never seen before.

Wishbone gazed up at her and wagged his tail politely. She tossed her colorfully embroidered shawl over one shoulder and smiled around the table. She had short, sleek reddish-blond hair and bright green eyes that flashed with a sense of adventure.

"While I was traveling down the Ganges in India," the young woman was saying, "we often camped out in the brush to watch the tigers hunt. The guide said it was too dangerous, but I told him I had a way with cats."

Wishbone growled. "Me too," he said. "You go on with your story. I'll track down the cat in here!"

Wishbone dropped to his stomach and crept under the table in search of his prey. "Closer, closer," he said. "I'm just about—" Wishbone jerked his head up in surprise. There on the floor beneath the young woman's chair sat a ball like none he had ever seen. It was the king of jingly balls. Wishbone couldn't tear his gaze away from it.

Fiery reds! Icy blues! Four or five inches across, with mirrors and sparkles, nubby rubber bumps, and satiny spots that made Wishbone long to push his muzzle against them.

Wishbone cocked his ears. He could almost hear the jingly ball cry out: "Bite me! Chew me! Shake me in your mouth!"

"Dinky! You've got to see this!" Wishbone took a step toward the ball and heard a low growl. He looked up to see a black Siamese cat in the young woman's lap, half-hidden by her shawl. Even so, Wishbone could tell that the feline was nearly his own size. The silky brown cat looked down on the ball with an air of possession that Wishbone could hardly make himself believe. This toy, this treasure among jingly balls, belonged to a . . . cat!

As Wishbone stared in horror, the cat jumped lightly down to the floor and laid a velvet paw on the ball.

A bell jingled faintly. It was calling to Wishbone! But the terrier didn't have a chance to get any closer. The cat delicately closed his teeth around one of the ball's rubbery bumps. Then he jumped back onto the young woman's lap, draped his paws down over her knees, and gazed at Wishbone with cool green eyes.

The fur along Wishbone's spine bristled. "That ball is far too large and grand for a mere cat like you."

Dinky obviously shared his opinion. The Chihuahua started to bark, yapping and jumping around the young woman's chair.

The woman glanced down at Wishbone and Dinky. "Midnight, have you been teasing these gentlemen?" she asked as she stroked the cat's head.

Midnight flicked his tail up so that it brushed against her chin. She smiled as if they were sharing a private joke.

"As a matter of fact, Madame," Wishbone said, "my friend Dinky and I are personal friends of the owners, and we'd like Midnight to leave."

Wishbone felt a tug on his collar. "Excuse me?" he cried. "I think you've got the wrong collar. Joe?" To Wishbone's amazement, Joe continued to pull him toward the door. "Joe, what has that feline menace done to you?"

"Sorry, boy," said Joe. "Midnight and Kayla are special guests at Pepper Pete's. You're a regular. I'll bring you back tomorrow."

Damont picked up Dinky and followed Joe and Wishbone to the door. "Don't worry, I'll get rid of him, Kayla," Damont called over his shoulder to the young woman.

"I shall return!" Wishbone barked out. "We have not yet begun to fight!"

Joe and Damont let the door close behind them before Wishbone could even finish his speech.

Chapter Two

Sam breathed a sigh of relief as she made her way around the table to where Jimmy was sitting. Thank goodness she'd found him!

She gave a quick wave to her dad, who was spooning sauce onto a flat circle of pizza dough behind the counter. Then she sat down next to Jimmy and asked, "Why didn't you wait for me at school?"

Jimmy barely glanced at her. He turned his baseball cap backward on his head and said, "I was busy." Then he turned quickly back to Kayla, who wore a tiger pendant with flashing emerald eyes.

"A tiger tried to attack my family when we went to Jungle World," Jimmy said. "I hypnotized him the way I saw a magician do in a movie."

Sam felt a twinge of irritation. Here she'd been going crazy trying to find him. And Jimmy had barely even bothered to answer her!

Too busy bragging, she thought. A tiger attack? Hypnotizing? Where did he come up with this stuff?

"Jimmy, that's impossible," David said.

"You can't hypnotize a tiger!"

"Actually," Kayla put in. "I've used that method myself. It works very well on cobras."

For a moment the table was silent as everyone turned to Kayla. Sam stared at the young woman. She actually sounded serious. But there was something more—something familiar about her. Sam remembered reading a magazine article about India, and tigers. . . .

"You're Kayla Cooper!" she exclaimed. "The globe-trotting heiress!"

Kayla smiled modestly. Sam was right!

"She's staying with my family for a few days," Isabel explained. "Kayla, I haven't introduced you to my friends Joe Talbot, David Barnes, and Sam Kepler. You already know Damont and Jimmy."

Sam felt a thrill run through her. She couldn't believe she was sitting at a table with the Kayla Cooper. Sam had seen Kayla in every newspaper and on every TV news show there was. No wonder she'd looked familiar! Kayla was only in her early twenties. But she had already traveled all over the world as an adventuress. According to the articles Sam had read, Kayla lived for excitement.

"I see my reputation precedes me," Kayla said with an easy laugh.

"I read all about your trek through Nepal," Sam told her. "And that kayaking trip through the rapids in the Grand Canyon." Sam grinned. "I hope I get to do something like that one day."

Kayla's green eyes gazed at Sam with new interest. "It's nice to meet someone else who has a taste for adventure," she said. "After all, the world is really just a big playground, right?" She shot Sam a wide smile, and Sam found herself smiling back right away.

Kayla reached down to pet the Siamese cat in her lap. "Maybe we'll go hot air ballooning over the Andes sometime," she said.

Sam laughed. "I guess," she agreed.

"Maybe after you're finished baby-sitting, Sam," Damont said with a sly grin.

His teasing comment reminded Sam that he was the one who was supposed to be watching Jimmy in the first place. She shot a sideways glance at him. If he was too busy to baby-sit, what was he doing here?

"So what's your big project, Damont?" she asked. "Trying out all the new toppings at Pepper Pete's?"

"Very funny." Damont leaned over the table toward her. "I'm working on something, all right. You just don't know what it is yet."

Jimmy turned in his chair. "It's top secret. Damont won't even tell me what it is," he said. "And I'm his partner. Right, Damont?"

"Really?" Kayla asked. "Sounds mysterious."

Damont shrugged and then changed the subject. "I read somewhere that you take your cat with you when you travel," he said to Kayla. "Is that true?"

Damont usually acted as if he were too cool for everyone and everything in Oakdale. But Sam noticed that even he was impressed by Kayla.

"Midnight is smarter than most people I know," Kayla said. "He and I have been friends for years. We're partners, too."

Jimmy brightened up. "Did Midnight help you train cobras?" he asked.

"I couldn't have done it without him," Kayla replied. "It was in Rajasthan. I used a special crystal pendulum that belonged to a maharajah."

"A crystal?" Jimmy said. "That's nothing. Guess what my family has?"

Kayla waited expectantly for the answer.

"A gold medallion!" Jimmy announced. "It's from the Civil War. Ulysses S. Grant gave it to my great-great-great . . . to one of my dad's ancestors."

Sam saw the way Damont rolled his eyes. Jimmy was obviously telling another tall tale. Still, Kayla at least had the grace to listen politely. She even acted interested.

"Really? Ulysses S. Grant?" Kayla said. "What does the medallion look like, Jimmy?"

"Well," said Jimmy, "it's—"

"Oh! Look at the time," Isabel's mother interrupted. "Kayla, I told Mrs. Hazlett we'd be back fifteen minutes ago. She must be wondering where we are."

Sam knew that Mrs. Hazlett was the housekeeper at the Ottingers' home, the sprawling stone house where Isabel and her parents lived with Isabel's great-grandfather, Carl Ottinger. The old man had lived in Oakdale practically forever. Sam had gotten to know him after an antique train belonging to him had mysteriously disappeared from Pepper Pete's.

"It was nice to meet you, Kayla," Sam said, as Kayla and the St. Clairs got to their feet.

She felt reluctant to say good-bye. Kayla was so

exotic and intriguing. Sam would have liked to keep talking to her. Then she remembered Jimmy. They would have to leave for dinner soon anyway.

"It was nice meeting all of you," Kayla said warmly. "I'd love to see you again before I leave."

She reached into her shoulder bag and pulled out some postcard-sized announcements. She handed them to Sam, Joe, David, Damont, and Jimmy. "The St. Clairs are giving a reception for me on Sunday," Kayla told them. "I hope you all can come."

Sam exchanged excited glances with Joe and David. "We'll definitely be there," she said. "Thanks!"

Kayla started to sling her bag over her shoulder, then paused. "Actually . . . I've got something you might like," she said slowly, looking right at Sam.

"Me?" Sam asked.

Kayla pulled a paperback book from her bag and handed it to Sam. The cover looked worn, and the pages were dog-eared.

"*The Amateur Cracksman*," Sam said, reading the title. "It looks like a mystery."

Kayla nodded. "It's a book of short stories written by a man named E.W. Hornung. He was the brother-in-law of Arthur Conan Doyle, believe it or not."

"The guy who wrote Sherlock Holmes?" Joe asked. He shot a look of fresh interest at the book in Sam's hands.

"That's right," Kayla said.

"What's a cracksman?" Sam asked.

"I don't want to give away anything," Kayla said, her green eyes shining. "Why don't you read the stories yourself and find out? I think you'll find that they

feature a very . . . different hero from Sherlock Holmes."

"Well, you've definitely made me curious," Sam said, laughing. "I guess I'll take you up on your offer, Kayla. Thanks."

"My pleasure," Kayla replied. "Bye, everyone."

"Jimmy?"

Sam looked up from the counter in the Kidds' kitchen an hour later. She'd only taken a few minutes to look at *The Amateur Cracksman* while the lasagna was heating up in the microwave. But that was all it had taken. Jimmy was nowhere in sight.

"Jimmy?" Sam said once more. She felt a stab of annoyance as she moved to the hall and called up the stairs. "Dinner's ready! Come downstairs, okay?"

Again there was no answer. Sam didn't find Jimmy in the living room, dining room, den, or in any of the upstairs bedrooms. "He's disappeared again," she sighed as she pushed open the kitchen door and headed outside.

It was starting to get dark. In the shadowy recesses beneath a maple tree, Sam saw the boxlike shape of a storage shed. The door was open, and Sam saw the yellow glow of a flashlight beam inside.

"Bingo," she whispered. The grass whipped against her sneakers as she strode across the yard to the shed.

"What are you doing out here, Jimmy?" she asked.

Jimmy pointed his flashlight right at Sam so she couldn't see anything. "Halt!" he called in a deep voice. "What's the password?"

Sam blinked, blocking the blinding light with her hands. "Password? How about 'lasagna'?" she said. She stepped into the shed, stooping so she wouldn't hit her head on the low doorway. "Come on, Jimmy. Dinner's ready and—"

Loud footsteps pounded along the ground behind her. The door to the shed slammed shut with a metallic bang!

Jimmy jumped. "Hey!" he cried.

Sam shot her hand out and pushed against the door. It didn't budge. She reached for the door handle, then realized there wasn't one.

Feeling a little panicky, Sam threw all of her weight against the door, but it remained firmly shut.

The footsteps outside retreated. Sam felt a shiver run through her as the sounds faded to silence. "Someone's locked us in!" she cried.

Chapter Three

"We're locked in?" Jimmy pushed past Sam and banged his flashlight against the shed door. "Who's out there? Let us out!" he cried.

"Open the door!" Sam called out.

Not a single sound came from the other side of the door. Whoever had locked them in was gone.

"W-what's going on?" Jimmy asked.

Goose bumps had popped out all over Sam's arms and legs. Her heart was pounding, but she didn't want Jimmy to see how nervous she was. He was just a kid—and she was responsible for him.

"Don't worry. We're going to get out of here," she said, trying to sound absolutely sure of herself. "Come on, help me push."

Jimmy's flashlight beam glowed yellow on his face. Sam was glad to see some of his uneasiness fade. He leaned against the door next to Sam. Together, they tried to force the door open, but the lock held firm.

"There must be another way," Sam murmured. "What kind of lock does the door have? Is there a key or a padlock?"

Jimmy shook his head. "Just a latch," he told her.

"Then we can release it . . . somehow." Sam turned around. It was so dark inside the shed that she couldn't see clearly. "Shine your flashlight around, okay?" she said.

As Jimmy moved the light across the shed, Sam kept her eyes on the items the beam lit up. "Rake . . . lawnmower . . .

"There!" She jumped toward some string and rope that were stuffed on a shelf along the side wall.

"What's that for?" Jimmy asked.

Sam took a ball of string from the pile. "We can feed the string through the crack at the top of the door," she said. Her mind raced as she thought out the possibilities. "All we need now is a piece of bent wire to put on the end. That will hook the latch when we lower the string—"

"I've got a fishing hook!" Jimmy sprang across the shed to the back wall. Sam caught sight of a couple of fishing rods leaning against the wall. On the floor next to them was a tackle box.

"Good idea," Sam said. "Get the biggest one you can find."

Jimmy hunched over the tackle box and shone his flashlight over the contents. Then he straightened up with a big smile. "How's this?" He held up a sturdy-looking fishing hook about an inch long.

"Perfect," Sam told him. "Let's give it a try."

Sam tied the hook to one end of the string. While Jimmy pushed against the shed door, Sam slid the hook through the crack and let out the string little by little. She heard a faint metallic pinging noise as the hook bounced against the door, but it didn't catch the latch.

Sam frowned. "Maybe I need to drop it lower," she said.

She let out some more string. Her breath caught in her throat as she felt the hook catch. *Please, let this work*, she thought. She gave a tug and—

Click! The latch released.

"We did it!" Jimmy whooped. He gave Sam a high five as she pushed open the door. "We make a great team," he said. "You can be my partner."

"Anytime." Sam laughed and dropped her arm around Jimmy's shoulders.

Her smile faded as she glanced at the lighted windows of Jimmy's house. "I hope everything is okay inside," she said.

"You think it was robbers?" Jimmy asked, hesitating. "Aliens?"

"I don't think we'll be visiting any other galaxies tonight," Sam murmured. She hesitated, her eyes still on the house. Should she call her dad? The police?

Don't jump to conclusions, she thought, shaking herself. *Everything looks fine. That was probably some prankster playing a joke on us.*

"Come on," she said, ruffling Jimmy's hair. "Let's just take a look around to make sure there aren't any extraterrestrials under the beds."

Nothing downstairs looked as if it had been disturbed. Still, Sam didn't completely relax until she and Jimmy had checked the upstairs bedrooms, too.

"This is the last room," she said, as she and Jimmy checked his parents' bedroom. "It doesn't look as if anybody's been in here."

She was just about to close the door when something on the dresser caught her eye. It was a medallion of gleaming, burnished gold, shaped in an oval, with flowery scrollwork around the edges. It hung by a faded, purple satin ribbon from the corner of a framed photograph. Sam walked over and picked it up. The inscription of fancy, old-fashioned letters read:

FOR COLONEL JEFFERSON KIDD,

with sincere gratitude for
devoted military service

ULYSSES S. GRANT

"Wow!" Sam said, brushing a finger over the gold. "This is the medallion you were talking about in Pepper Pete's. The one Ulysses S. Grant gave to your relative?"

"Jefferson Kidd," Jimmy supplied. "That's him there." He nodded at the framed, sepia-colored photograph from which the medallion had been hanging. "Isn't it cool?"

"Definitely," Sam said. "To be honest, I thought you were making it up. It sounded so valuable I couldn't believe you had it in your house."

Jimmy's brown eyes gleamed with excitement as he looked up at her. "It's handed down from father to son," he said. "That means I get it next!"

"Well, take care of it," Sam told him. "I wish we had something like this in my family." Giving the medallion a last look, she hung it back over the photograph of Jefferson Kidd and headed for the hall.

"My dad's going to hand me down his special

pizza recipes," she said, grinning. "Let's eat!"

"Good-bye, Mr. Kidd. 'Night, Jimmy," Sam said an hour later as she stepped out the Kidds' front door.

"Good night, Sam. Thanks again," Mr. Kidd said.

Sam waved, then strapped on her helmet, got on her bike, and started down the driveway. What a day, she thought. Everything had turned out all right in the end. But after losing Jimmy and getting locked in that shed, she was glad to be heading home.

"Sam! Wait!" A cry came from across the street.

Sam squeezed the brakes and looked at the stone house where Isabel lived. The place was so huge and old that it reminded Sam of a castle.

"Hi, Isabel. Hi, Kayla!" Sam called back. She rode up the curved driveway to where Kayla and Isabel were just getting off their bikes.

"So our paths cross again," Kayla said. She wore a sleek athletic jumpsuit. Taking off her safety helmet, she shook out her short hair.

Sam nodded at Kayla's bike. "Did you two just finish a ride?" she asked.

"I took Kayla on a bicycle tour. Oakdale by night," Isabel said. "Actually, we spent more time talking than looking at the sights. Guess what? I'm writing an article on Kayla for the *Oakdale Chronicle*! Do you want to work on it with me?"

"Definitely," Sam said immediately. Writing for the town paper was a big opportunity. She'd have the chance to get to know Kayla better, too—and to hear about more of her adventures.

Just thinking about it made Sam happy.

Kayla smiled warmly at Sam. "I don't usually do interviews, but I'll make an exception for this one."

"We'll talk more about it tomorrow, all right?" Isabel added. "We're meeting Wanda at the *Chronicle* office at ten o'clock." Wanda Gilmore was the Talbots' next-door neighbor and the owner of the *Chronicle.*

"Great," Sam said. "See you there!"

The smile didn't leave Sam's face during the entire ride back to her house. She couldn't wait to get to the *Chronicle* office in the morning. And in the meantime I have a new book to read, she reminded herself.

As soon as Sam got home, she settled onto the living room couch with *The Amateur Cracksman*. Within minutes, she was caught up in the first story, "The Ides of March."

The story took place in London, England, in the late 1800s. The narrator, a young man named Bunny, was a member of the high society who had squandered his inheritance. He turned for help to his old chum, A. J. Raffles.

They had met at boarding school, where Raffles was a top cricket player and Bunny the devoted younger classmate who idolized him. Raffles agreed to help Bunny with his money problems in return for his absolute loyalty.

Bunny was shocked to learn that his good friend Raffles had a dark secret. He was really a notorious cat burglar!

So that's what an amateur cracksman is, Sam mused, as she came to the end of the story. A gentleman thief!

Sam was just starting the second story when the door opened and her dad walked in. "Hi, honey," he greeted her. "How was baby-sitting?"

"Harder than I expected," she admitted as she put her book down. "And something kind of strange happened."

Her dad's face grew serious as she told him about how she and Jimmy had been locked in the shed. "I still don't know who locked us in," she finished. "But we got out and everything was fine."

"That's great, Sam," her dad told her. "But—"

The ringing of the phone interrupted him. Sam headed for the extension in the kitchen and answered it.

"Sam?" Mr. Kidd's voice came over the line. "I need to talk to you."

Mr. Kidd sounded very serious and upset. "What's wrong, Mr. Kidd?" she asked.

"It's Jefferson Kidd's gold medallion," Jimmy's father began. There was a slight pause before Mr. Kidd continued. "It's missing, Sam."

"What?" Sam gasped. "That's impossible!"

"Jimmy says you and he were looking at it," Mr. Kidd went on. "I was hoping you could come over and help us figure out what happened."

Sam's answer was immediate. "I'll do everything I can," she offered. "I'm on my way, Mr. Kidd."

Chapter Four

"Hi, Dinky." Wishbone wagged his tail and trotted across the Kidds' front yard. "What's up?"

He and Dinky had already had lots of fun that day. After being put out of Pepper Pete's, they had chased squirrels and dug at the roots of their favorite trees in Jackson Park. Then they had explored some new scents in the backyards of some of their canine pals around town. Oh, to be a dog running free in Oakdale! What could be better?

It was only when Wishbone's stomach alarm clock went off that he'd gone home for his evening kibble. Now he was ready to pick up where he and Dinky had left off. "Ready?" He sniffed at Dinky's nose. "Let's go!"

The two dogs were just trotting down the street when a familiar car passed them and turned into the Kidds' driveway.

"Hi, Sam! Hi, Walter!" Wishbone called.

His ears perked up when he saw a second car pull into the driveway and park. "Police?" Wishbone gazed at the uniformed officer behind the wheel.

"Let's check it out, Dinky."

The two dogs ran back to the Kidds' house at top speed. They reached the front door just as Sam, her dad, and the police officer met on the front steps.

"I appreciate your coming over here on such short notice," the stocky officer told Sam and her dad. The officer leaned forward to press the doorbell.

"We're glad to help," Sam's father said. "We want to find that missing medallion. Sam tells me it's a family heirloom."

"Missing? Is there a thief in the neighborhood?" Wishbone shot an alarmed glance at the police officer, whom he knew from around Oakdale. "Don't leave Tracking Dog out of the loop, Officer Krulla. What am I sniffing out?"

Just then the door was opened by Jimmy's father. He was a tall, dark-haired man wearing a suit. He had the same boyish face as Jimmy, but he looked worried. "Thanks for coming," Mr. Kidd said.

Jimmy's father showed everyone into the living room. Wishbone saw that Jimmy was there, sitting on the sofa.

"I'm so sorry about the medallion, Mr. Kidd," Sam said as she and her father sat down next to Jimmy. "What happened?"

"All I know for sure is that the medallion was missing when I came home," Jimmy's father said. "Apparently Jimmy and Sam were the last ones to see it."

Wishbone sat down on the carpet near Sam. He gazed at the people around him. "This sounds like a case for Tracking Dog, all right! Now, what did the missing item smell like?"

Officer Krulla took a seat on an armchair across from the sofa. He took out a notebook and pen and then turned to Jimmy's father. "Why don't you tell us how you discovered the medallion was missing?" he said.

"I went upstairs to change after Sam left," Mr. Kidd began. "I saw right away that the medallion was not hanging from the picture frame on the dresser. I asked Jimmy about it. Sometimes he likes to play with it," he said, shooting Jimmy a stern look.

"No way!" Jimmy spoke up right away. "All I did was tell Sam about it."

"That's right," Sam agreed.

Sam went on to tell everyone about being locked in the shed with Jimmy. Wishbone perked up his ears when Sam explained how they had managed to get out right away.

"Leave it to Sam to find her way out of a jam." Wishbone wagged his tail, smiling up at her. "Way to go!"

"When we got out, the first thing I did was check the house to make sure everything was okay," Sam went on. "That's when I saw the medallion, up in the bedroom."

"Sam really liked it," Jimmy said, sitting up straighter on the sofa. "She said I should be sure to take care of it." He turned to Sam, his dark eyes shining. "You said you wished you had something like that in your family, remember, Sam?"

"Yeah, it was really neat," Sam said.

Wishbone saw a slight tightening in Mr. Kidd's jaw muscle as he glanced at Sam. Officer Krulla jotted something down in his notebook. Then he turned to Sam and said, "What happened after Jimmy showed you the medallion?"

Sam shrugged. "Nothing," she answered. "We went downstairs to have dinner. When we left the bedroom the medallion was right where we found it, hanging from the photograph of Jefferson Kidd."

Officer Krulla's face remained very serious. "What about after that, Sam?" he asked. "Did you see the medallion again before Mr. Kidd came home?"

Sam shook her head.

"Did anyone else come into the house?" Officer Krulla asked. "Maybe someone could have come in when you were busy somewhere else?"

Sam thought a moment. "I don't see how. Jimmy and I were downstairs in the kitchen after that," she said. "We were there until Mr. Kidd came home."

Sam twisted the ends of her blond hair between her fingers, frowning. "The stairs were in plain sight the whole time," she added. "I definitely would have seen anyone who tried to sneak up to the bedroom."

"So . . ." Officer Krulla said, keeping his eyes on Sam, "no one else was here. You're sure of it?"

"I'm positive," Sam said firmly.

Officer Krulla wrote again in his notebook, then snapped it shut and got to his feet. "Maybe the medallion was misplaced," he suggested. "I'd like to take a look around upstairs."

"Good idea!" Wishbone trotted eagerly toward the steps with Officer Krulla. "It's time for Tracking Dog to investigate the crime scene!"

Jimmy's father led the way upstairs. Wishbone followed on his heels, along with everyone else. When they reached Mr. and Mrs. Kidd's bedroom,

Wishbone put his paws up on the dresser and took a good sniff at the photograph of Jimmy's Civil War relative. The gold medallion was nowhere to be seen.

"What about that window?" Walter suggested. He pointed toward a half-opened window near the bed. "Isn't that a tree outside? Could someone have climbed in?"

Trotting over, Wishbone jumped up and rested his front paws against the windowsill. He had no trouble spotting the maple tree in the evening darkness. Its lower branches looked thick and sturdy. But the branches at second-story level were no thicker than a dog biscuit.

Officer Krulla looked out the window beside Wishbone. "The only branch near the window is too small to support a person's weight," he said. He straightened up, tapping his notebook with his pen. "The thief had to have come up from downstairs."

Wishbone saw Sam's puzzled expression as she gazed at the slender branches of the tree outside. "I don't get it. There's no way in from up here. And no way anyone could have snuck up from downstairs without us seeing. How did the thief do it?"

No one answered Sam's question. At least not out loud. But Wishbone noticed that all the adult eyes in the room flicked uncomfortably toward Sam.

"Wait a minute," Sam said, taking a step backward. "You don't think I had anything to do with this, do you?"

Wishbone saw the look of surprise—and hurt—on her face. "My pal Sam, a thief? Never!" he said emphatically.

Apparently, Jimmy agreed with him. "Sam and I already told you, Dad. We left the medallion right here on the dresser," he said.

Jimmy's father didn't look convinced. "I'm sorry, Sam," he said. "I just don't understand who else could have taken it."

Before Sam's father could say anything, Officer Krulla held up a hand and said, "We don't have any suspects yet. The Oakdale police department will be doing all we can to find the thief and recover the medallion."

"So will Tracking Dog!" Wishbone barked his promise, wagging his tail. "Don't worry, Sam. I'll sniff out the real thief!"

Wishbone heard Dinky's dog door swish open and shut downstairs. "Good idea, Dinky. Let's go outside to look for clues."

Wishbone trotted downstairs and leaped through Dinky's doggie door onto the grass outside. He spotted the dark, square shape of the storage shed immediately.

"Hmm . . ." Wishbone trotted toward the shed. "I'll just sniff around and—"

Suddenly the Chihuahua's urgent barking rang out from the other side of the house.

"I'm on my way, Dinky!" Making an about-face, Wishbone raced toward the front yard. He rounded the side of Jimmy's house and saw Dinky across the street. The Chihuahua was on the grass next to the curved drive that led to Isabel's big stone house. Spotlights lit up the wide front lawn where Dinky jumped wildly about, barking at . . .

"That cat!" Wishbone growled.

His fur stood on end as he watched Midnight. The cat was just a few feet from Dinky, playing with . . . "The ball!"

Wishbone caught a tantalizing glimpse of color and sparkles as the cat batted the ball across the grass. It rolled temptingly close to Dinky. But before the Chihuahua could get a paw on the ball, Midnight batted it farther away.

"That cat doesn't deserve such a fine piece of plastic," Wishbone said, coming up beside Dinky.

Seeing Wishbone approach, Midnight arched his back and mockingly stretched himself. He reached out a silky paw and began nonchalantly to clean his ear.

"That ball was meant for us, Dinky!" Wishbone said. "Stick with me. We're going to get it."

The front door opened behind Midnight and

Kayla peered out. Her eyes narrowed when she saw Wishbone and Dinky. She nodded to the two dogs and then let out a low whistle. "Come in, Midnight. Time for your supper."

Midnight calmly picked up his jingly ball with his teeth and went to the front door.

Kayla paused in the doorway, turned, and smiled at Wishbone and Dinky. "Better luck next time, boys," she said. Her sly smile stayed in Wishbone's mind long after she shut the door.

"She's going to be trouble, Dinky," he warned his friend. "But she's no match for us. By this time tomorrow we'll be fetching that jingly ball as dogs were meant to do!" Wishbone trotted over to the Chihuahua and touched noses. "I've got a plan!"

"Thanks for coming over, guys," Sam said. She opened the front door and led Joe and David into her house. She had called them as soon as she and her dad had gotten home from the Kidds'. It was getting late, but after what had just happened, she wanted to be with her friends.

Joe shook his head as he and David slung their jackets over the closet doorknob. "I can't believe they think you stole the medallion."

"They obviously don't know you very well," David added.

"No one accused me, exactly," Sam said, as she led the way to the kitchen. "But it was pretty obvious I'm the only suspect."

Sam sighed. It was good to know her friends were

on her side. But she couldn't erase the image of Officer Krulla and Jimmy's father looking at her as if she were a criminal. Every time she pictured their doubtful glances, it made her feel awful—and all the more resolved to find the real thief.

Her father was just pouring hot cocoa into four steaming mugs at the kitchen counter. "Hi, guys," he greeted the boys. "Help yourselves."

"Thanks, Mr. Kepler," Joe said. As they sat down at the table, he turned to Sam. "David and I were talking on the way over. We think you need to find the real thief. Then you'll be off the hook."

Sam wrapped her hands around her warm mug. "That's exactly what I was thinking," she said. "But whoever it is got in and out of the house while I was right there. Jimmy and I didn't see or hear a thing, and the police didn't find a single clue. This is no ordinary thief."

"Couldn't the thief have taken the medallion after you left?" David suggested.

"There wasn't enough time," Sam told him. "Mr. Kidd said he went up to his room right after I left, and the medallion was gone." She took a sip of her cocoa. "It had to have happened when I was there."

Sam's father reached over to squeeze her shoulder. "It's not your fault, Sam."

"I know that," she said. "We just have to prove it to everyone else."

Sam saw Joe's eyes on her copy of *The Amateur Cracksman*, which lay on the kitchen table. He opened the book to the spot she had marked with the invitation to

Kayla's reception. "You already started reading this, huh?"

"Yeah. They're not your typical mysteries," she said.

"What do you mean?" David asked.

Sam told them about A. J. Raffles and his friend Bunny. "They mix with England's high society," Sam explained. "But when they need money, they steal jewelry from the high society types they know."

"Wow," Joe laughed. "Is Raffles the hero?"

"Yes," Sam said. "He's very likable, even though he's a thief. That's the strange thing."

"Does anyone know what Raffles is up to?" David asked, looking across the table at Sam.

"No way," she said, shaking her head. "That's part of his game, playing the role of society gentleman and top cricket player while all the time he's planning a great jewel heist."

David plunked his mug down on the table. "Now we have our own thief to worry about," he said, "right here in Oakdale."

Chapter Five

Sam breathed deeply as she walked through the crisp autumn sunshine toward the *Oakdale Chronicle* building on Saturday morning. She'd stayed up late the night before, reading some more of the stories in *The Amateur Cracksman*. The stories had helped take her mind off the missing medallion. But now, thoughts about the theft came swirling back into her head.

How could she be the top suspect? It was so unfair!

Sam took another deep breath. The fresh air helped to clear her mind. She was glad she'd be busy talking to Wanda about the article she and Isabel were writing on Kayla. She needed to concentrate on something—anything-besides that medallion.

She opened the front door to the *Chronicle* building and stepped inside. The desks at the front of the office were empty. But Sam heard voices coming from Wanda's balcony office at the back of the building.

"Hello?" she called.

"Hi, Sam. Come on up!" Wanda's slender,

pixie-ish face appeared above the balcony railing. She smiled down at Sam and waved her toward the stairs that led up to her office. "Kayla and Isabel are already here."

Wanda's energy and enthusiasm had a way of rubbing off onto the people around her. As Sam climbed the stairs to the balcony office, she saw that Isabel and Kayla were already caught up in the project. They both smiled at Sam as they sorted through the many photographs and newspaper and magazine articles that covered Wanda's desk.

Sam heard a jingling sound at her feet. Looking down, she saw Midnight batting his big colorful ball across the floor of the loft. "Hi, Midnight. Are you here to help, too?" she asked.

"Absolutely." Kayla let her embroidered shawl drop onto the chair back behind her. She grinned at Sam and said, "Any article about me would have to include my partner, right?"

Sam took off her jacket and hung it over the back of the only empty chair. "Wow," she said, gazing at the dozens of articles on Wanda's desk. "Are all these about you, Kayla?"

Kayla nodded. "People do seem to find me interesting," she said with a laugh. Picking up a handful of articles, she let them shower back down onto the desk. "I hear people are interested in you these days, too."

"Mr. Kidd told us about the Civil War medallion being stolen while you were baby-sitting, Sam," Isabel added.

Sam felt her frustration come flooding back.

"Then I guess he told you that I'm his top suspect," she said.

"You?" Wanda asked, her eyes filled with surprise and concern.

Sam nodded. "The police can't figure out how anyone could have gotten in without leaving any clues and without being seen by Jimmy or me," she said. "If no one else could have done it, that leaves me."

"That's ridiculous!" Kayla said, shaking her head.

"Not to mention frustrating," Sam added. "Anyway, I figure the best way to clear my name is to find the real thief." She pulled the empty chair back with a determined tug and sat down. "In the meantime, I'm going to work on this article."

"That's the spirit," Kayla said, her green eyes sparkling. "It's a point of honor not to take the blame for something that the thief did."

Kayla's eyes focused on something on Wanda's desk. Following her gaze, Sam saw a glass display cube. Inside was a man's ring with a thick gold band and a large red stone set in the middle of it.

"Hey, what's that, Miss Gilmore?" Sam asked.

"This?" Wanda lifted the top of the cube and took the ring from its base. "It belonged to my father. He made the *Oakdale Chronicle* what it is today."

"That looks like a ruby," Isabel said, pointing at the sparkling red stone in the center of the ring.

Kayla leaned forward to get a closer look. "It's beautiful," she said. "I love the design on the band. Art Deco, isn't it?"

"That's right," Wanda replied, turning the ring

over in her hand. "My father had it made when he first took over the *Chronicle*, back in the nineteen-twenties. I keep it here for sentimental reasons. I guess I feel it's good luck."

"Miss Gilmore," Kayla said suddenly. "Maybe you should put it somewhere safe until this thief is caught."

Wanda tapped a finger against the ring, then nodded. "You might be right," she said. "I'll take this over to the bank later and put it in my safe-deposit box."

"Good idea," Sam agreed. She gave a shiver as she stared at the ring. "I'd hate to see the thief get away with anything else."

Wishbone wagged his tail and gazed through the front windows of the *Oakdale Chronicle* office. "They're coming out, Dinky!"

Dinky danced from paw to paw on the sidewalk behind him. The Chihuahua was too short to see through the window. But Wishbone—with his paws pressed against the bottom ledge and his nose against the glass—had been keeping a close canine eye on the activity inside.

He jumped down to the sidewalk. "Here's our chance!"

Wishbone saw Dan Bloodgood, the mailman, drive past in his mailcart. He barked a quick hello. Wishbone knew Ellen and Joe were in town shopping, along with dozens of other friends and neighbors whom he recognized. But the terrier had been too busy to make his usual rounds. He and Dinky had been stationed outside the newspaper office ever since Wishbone had seen Midnight and his jingly ball go inside with Kayla.

"When Midnight comes out, we'll ambush him," Wishbone instructed the small dog.

Wishbone crouched low over his front paws as the door opened a moment later. Sam came out first, zipping up her jacket. Isabel was right behind her. Then Kayla stepped onto the sidewalk, pulling her shawl around her shoulders. Wanda stood behind, holding the door open for someone.

"I've sighted the enemy!" Wishbone inched forward as Midnight stepped gracefully through the doorway. The large Siamese paused, blinking into the fall sunshine. The mere sight of the jingly ball in his teeth made Wishbone itch to bite it himself.

A second later he had his chance. Midnight dropped the ball to the sidewalk. "Dinky, now!" Wishbone barked loudly.

Dinky ran up from behind. Midnight swished his tail calmly out of the Chihuahua's reach. The cat's cool green eyes followed the jingly ball as it rolled down the sidewalk.

"Back so soon, boys?" Kayla said.

Wishbone jumped closer to Midnight, keeping up a steady stream of barking. "Now go for the ball, Dinky. Go!"

Dinky raced toward the jingly ball as fast as his tiny legs would take him. Within moments he was closing in on the ball. . . .

"Hey!" Wishbone yelped as Kayla's colorful shawl

fell over Dinky.

"Gotcha!" Kayla murmured.

Wishbone saw a Dinky-sized lump in the shawl. Dinky's nose turned this way and that beneath the fabric.

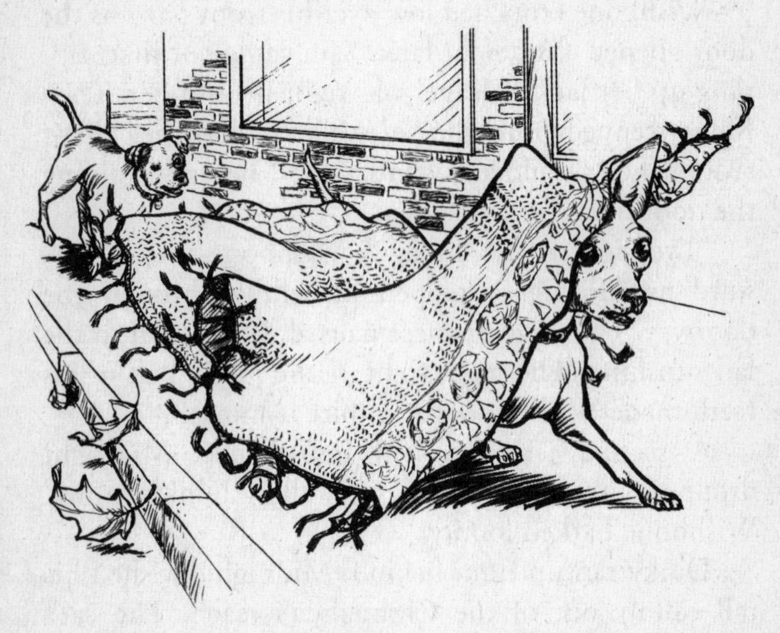

"Give up, boys?" Kayla asked. She stepped calmly past Wishbone and picked up Midnight's jingly ball by one of its rubbery bumps.

"Kayla!" Isabel cried out suddenly. "Dinky's running away with your shawl!"

Sure enough, Dinky was racing down Oak Street. Wishbone could see he was trying to shake the shawl off. But the cloth was caught on the little dog's head. As he ran down Oak Street, Dinky dragged the shawl behind him. He bumped into a woman pushing a stroller, then ran blindly on.

"Wait up!" Wishbone raced after the Chihuahua.

Kayla's laugh rang out behind Wishbone. "He looks like a shawl with feet!" she said.

Looking back, Wishbone saw that Kayla and the two girls were running after Dinky, too. Wanda stayed behind just long enough to lock the front door to the *Chronicle* office. Then she, too, joined the chase.

"Look out for cars!" Wishbone called as Dinky ran down the street. Just then he saw Joe step out of Oakdale Sports & Games up ahead. His mother, Ellen Talbot, was right behind him. "Joe! Ellen! I need backup here!"

Joe frowned. His eyes flicked from Dinky, to Wishbone, to the crowd of people running behind them. Dinky was moving fast. But Joe reached down and caught a corner of Kayla's shawl in his fingertips. A moment later, Dinky and the shawl were safely in his arms.

"Thanks, buddy!" Wishbone jumped around Joe's feet, barking.

"I'm glad you were there, Joe," Sam said, as everyone came running up.

"We heard all the barking," Ellen said, her face filled with concern. "Is everything all right?"

Joe finished untangling the shawl from around Dinky's head and tail. Then he placed Dinky gently on the sidewalk next to Wishbone. "I thought I heard Wishbone," he said. He handed Kayla her shawl, then scratched Wishbone behind his ears. "What's the matter, boy?"

"If I didn't know better, I'd say Wishbone and Dinky tried to ambush Midnight," Sam explained.

"Iggy and Axel did the same thing when Kayla and Midnight arrived yesterday," Isabel said, with a knowing nod. "It got so bad Dad decided to put them in a kennel until after Kayla and Midnight leave."

Wishbone barked up at Isabel. "So that's why my buddies weren't at Pepper Pete's yesterday."

"Where is Midnight?" Joe wondered, looking around.

Wishbone turned his head to look up and down Oak Street. He didn't see Midnight—or his awesome jingly ball—anywhere.

"We must have left him at the Chronicle," Wanda said. She shot a searching glance across the street in the direction of the newspaper office.

Kayla brushed off her shawl and wrapped it around her shoulders. "Midnight won't go far," she said, glancing at him and Dinky. "Now that things have calmed down, I'm sure he's waiting for us."

"I'll help you look for him," Joe offered.

"I'd like to help, but I've got to get to the grocery store," Ellen said. "I'll see you back at the house, Joe."

Wishbone barked his good-bye along with everyone else. As the rest of them started back toward the *Chronicle* office, Wishbone was on red alert. Up ahead, sunlight glinted off the windows of the newspaper office. Wishbone didn't see any sign of Midnight. But as he passed the dark, narrow alley behind the *Chronicle* building, something made him stop.

Wishbone turned to stare down the alley—then froze with his paws on the sidewalk. "Hey! Who's that?"

He barked, sounding the alarm. "Wanda! Joe! Someone's sneaking around back there!"

"Wishbone? What's the matter, boy?" Sam asked. She stopped and turned to look at Wishbone. He stood at the end of the alleyway next to the *Chronicle* building. His barking sounded so urgent that she and Joe jogged over.

Sam peered into the alley—then gasped. "Someone's back there!"

She saw the flash of an arm as someone disappeared behind the building. The sounds of pounding footsteps echoed off the alley walls.

"The person is running away!" Joe shouted. "Come on!"

Just as they started to run, another voice came out of nowhere. "What's going on?"

Sam was surprised to see Jimmy Kidd come up beside her. But there was no time to answer his question. She took off down the alley after Joe. Sam had almost reached him when she felt a push from behind. The next thing she knew, her sneaker caught on the foot of whoever had pushed her and—

"Whoa!" Sam went flying. Her shoulder jammed into Joe's side, throwing him off balance. Seconds later, she, Joe, and Jimmy were lying in a tangled heap on the damp, packed dirt of the alley.

"Are you three all right?" Wanda's worried voice came from above them.

Sam blinked and looked up. Wanda, Kayla, and Isabel were bent over them. Wishbone and Dinky were there, too. Wishbone licked Joe's face.

Kayla leaned down and helped Sam to her feet. "All your parts still in working order?"

"I-I think so," Sam reported, still feeling a little dazed.

"I'm fine, too," Joe added. "How about you, Jimmy?"

Jimmy nodded, jumping to his feet. "Is the thief back there?" he asked, staring deeper into the alley. "Did we catch him?"

The thief! Sam snapped back into action. "Not yet," she said. "But I'm not giving up."

Sam ran down the alley and heard the others following her. When she reached the back of the *Chronicle* building, she peered along the rear wall. She didn't see anyone, but the metal frame of a fire escape partially blocked her view.

"I'll check the fire escape. You guys check the rest of the alley," she called.

Sam's sneakers thumped on the fire escape, sending a metallic echo through the alley. She climbed up to the second floor, but no one was there. The windows were protected by gates with metal bars. She tugged on one of the bars, but they were firmly locked in place. She looked up, but the fire escape didn't reach to the roof. Whoever she'd seen couldn't have escaped that way.

"Nothing?" Isabel called from below.

Sam leaned over the railing and shook her head, then climbed back down to join Isabel. Up ahead Sam could see where the alley opened onto a side street. Joe, Wanda, Jimmy, and Kayla were standing there, shaking their heads.

"Whoever it was is gone," Joe said as they came back. He wiped at the mud on the leg of his jeans. "Too bad we got tripped up. What happened, anyway?"

Sam pushed aside her frustration and tried to figure it out. "I tripped over Jimmy's foot, I think. But . . ." Sam turned to Jimmy. "Where did you come from, Jimmy? You appeared totally out of the blue."

"I was looking for Damont," he answered. "We were in Oakdale Sports and Games. But Damont left without telling me. When I went out to look for him, I saw you guys and I knew something was up. I wanted to help."

Sam couldn't help thinking that his "help" was what had allowed the person to escape. But Jimmy had meant well. Somehow she mustered a smile and said, "Thanks, Jimmy. But it looks like whoever it was got away. . . ."

Sam let her voice trail off as she caught sight of something—sneaker prints in the mud. They had a distinctive swirl at the ball of the foot, like a cyclone. There were lots of the prints near the fire escape.

"Check it out," she said, pointing at the prints. "Whoever we saw back here was hanging around right here." She gazed up at the safety gates that covered the rear windows. "Is there any way inside from the fire escape?"

"No," Wanda answered. "The protective gates can't be opened from the outside. I locked the front door, too."

Sam tried to shake off the uneasy feeling that had come over her. Everyone else seemed nervous, too. No one spoke as they all walked back to the front of the building. Wanda tested the front door—and let out a relieved sigh.

"Still locked," she said. "So far, so good."

As Wanda turned the key in the lock, a faint jingling noise made Sam look down. "There's Midnight!" she announced.

The Siamese cat was walking down the sidewalk toward them with the jingly ball in his teeth.

"Hello, partner." Kayla scooped up the cat.

Wanda pushed open the front door to the newspaper office and stepped inside. Sam went in behind her, along with everyone else. Wishbone and Dinky trotted in at their feet.

Sam was relieved to see that the front desks looked exactly as they had earlier.

"I guess I was worried for nothing," Wanda said, smiling. She moved quickly up the stairs toward her balcony office. "Everything seems to be—"

Wanda broke off in mid-sentence. She stopped short on the top step, and her hand flew to her mouth. "Oh, no!"

The tone of her voice told Sam something was very, very wrong.

"What is it, Miss Gilmore?" Sam raced up the steps—then drew her breath in sharply.

The glass display cube had been knocked from its

base. It lay on its side on the desktop. Both the cube and the base were empty.

"Your father's ruby ring," Sam whispered. "It's gone!"

Chapter Seven

Wishbone's nails clicked on the steps as he ran up to Wanda's balcony office. He squeezed in between Wanda and Sam, then jumped onto one of the chairs next to the desk. The glass cube lay on its side in front of Wishbone's muzzle, empty.

"I knew I should have taken it to the bank sooner," Wanda said. She gazed in shock at the empty cube. "Now it's gone!"

The others crowded around the desk behind Wishbone, all talking at once.

"But how did the thief get in and out?" Sam asked. Wishbone saw the puzzled expression on her face as she looked around. "The front door was locked. So were the gates over the windows on the fire escape."

Wishbone gazed up at the windows along the back wall of Wanda's balcony office. Only one window was open, he saw. A security gate outside barred any entrance.

"Maybe there's another open window?" Isabel suggested.

Wanda shook her head. "This is the only one I opened."

Kayla placed Midnight gently on a plush upholstered chair near the top of the balcony stairs. "Does anyone else have a key?" she asked, running a hand thoughtfully through her short hair.

Wanda shook her head again. Putting his muzzle to the ground, Wishbone began sniffing. "Tracking Dog is on the case. But . . . where are the clues?"

"It's just like what happened last night when Mr. Kidd's medallion was taken," Sam said. "The thief managed something that just doesn't seem possible."

"He did it again!" Jimmy agreed.

"But how?" said Kayla. "The thief certainly is clever."

"At least this time you were with us, Sam," Joe pointed out. "Now the police will know you're not the thief."

Sam gave a relieved nod. "There's something else, too. This time the thief left a trace," she said. She seemed deep in thought as she went over to the open window and looked down into the alley. "Those sneaker prints are really distinctive."

Wishbone trotted over to Wanda and put his paw on her hand. "Don't worry, Wanda. We'll catch the thief."

"Wishbone," Wanda said, frowning. "If you and Dinky hadn't chased Midnight and run off with Kayla's shawl, the thief wouldn't have had a chance to steal my father's ruby ring."

"But . . . chasing cats is a dog thing," Wishbone tried to explain. "Like burying bones and being faithful friends. It's what we do!"

Wanda reached for the phone on her desk. "I'd better call the police. Joe? Jimmy? Would you please take Wishbone and Dinky outside? I don't want them disturbing anything before the police get here."

“Sure, Miss Gilmore,” Joe said.

Out of the corner of his eye, Wishbone saw Midnight stretch out on Wanda’s plush chair. He batted his jingly ball gently from paw to paw, blinking blandly at Wishbone.

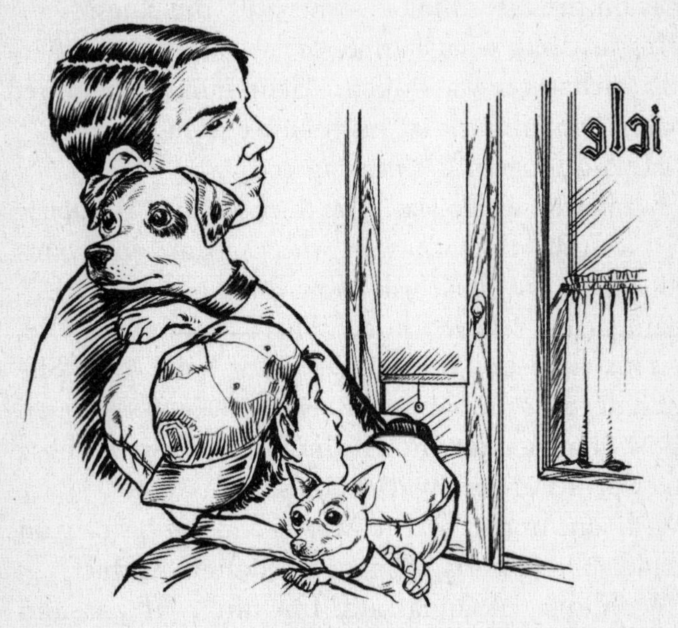

“I’ll be back!” Wishbone declared. But no one seemed to hear him. Jimmy picked up Dinky and headed for the door.

“Come on, Wishbone. Let’s go. “Joe gave Wishbone a pat, urging him down the balcony stairs.

“I’ll go, too,” Sam said. She headed for the steps behind Joe. “Good luck, Miss Gilmore.”

Wishbonc shot a final, longing glance at Midnight’s jingly ball. “We’ll find the thief!” he called.

Dinky barked his agreement from Jimmy’s arms.

But Wishbone lost his ally a moment later. With a quick good-bye to Sam and Joe, Jimmy and Dinky walked off down the street.

"We were only out of the newspaper office for a few minutes," Sam said.

"Thanks to Wishbone and Dinky." Joe angled a concerned look down at Wishbone.

"And Midnight!" Wishbone said. "Everyone keeps forgetting Midnight!" Wishbone paused to sniff the air. "Hmmm. What's that smell?" he wondered.

As he trotted forward once more, the faint scent grew stronger. Wishbone looked from side to side, searching for the source of the interesting aroma. "Joe! Sam! I just caught a whiff of something familiar. . . ."

Sam put her hands in her jacket pockets as she walked away from the newspaper office with Joe and Wishbone. "That's two thefts in less than twenty-four hours," she said.

"And practically no clues," Joe added.

Sam took a deep breath, trying to shake off the unsettled feeling that had come over her. Even Wishbone seemed agitated, she thought. His tail was stiff. He kept turning his head in different directions and sniffing the air.

As Sam watched, Wishbone barked and ran toward the pay phone outside Rosie's Rendezvous Books. Damont was on the phone. As Wishbone approached and sniffed at his sneakers, Damont frowned down at him.

"There's Damont," Sam said, pointing. "He

doesn't seem too happy to see Wishbone."

Still talking on the phone, Damont was trying to shoo Wishbone away with his feet. When he saw Sam and Joe coming up behind Wishbone, his whole expression changed. He spoke a few hurried words into the receiver and then slammed the phone down. Hoisting the strap of his backpack higher on his shoulder, he walked quickly down the sidewalk away from Joe and Sam. But Sam had already seen the guilty look that had flashed across his face.

"What's he hiding?" she wondered out loud.

She squinted, watching him closely. Wishbone also seemed interested in Damont. He followed closely on the boy's heels, barking and sniffing at his feet.

"Joe!" Sam cried. "Look at Damont's sneakers."

"Whoa." Joe gave a nod, his eyes widening. "And check out the prints he left by the phone booth!"

Sam had already seen the prints. Each one had a distinctive swirl at the ball of the foot. "I think we know who was in the alley. Come on. Let's go talk to him," she said.

Her whole body jolted to hyperawareness. They were finally getting somewhere!

She and Joe caught up to Damont as he rounded the corner past Pepper Pete's Pizza Parlor. Wishbone was still sniffing at Damont's sneakers. When he saw Sam and Joe, he let out a bark and wagged his tail.

"Hey, Damont," Sam said, coming up next to him. "Can we talk to you?"

"I'm kind of busy," he said without stopping.

Joe stepped quickly up to Damont's other side.

"Doing what? Hanging around behind the *Chronicle* building?" he asked.

Sam thought she saw a flash of guilt in Damont's eyes. But it was gone before she could be sure.

"Why would I hang out there?" Damont asked.

He was obviously trying to avoid them. But Sam wasn't going to let him get away with it! "Someone stole a gold-and-ruby ring from Miss Gilmore," she told him. "And there were sneaker prints like yours behind Miss Gilmore's office."

Damont shrugged. "Then there must be someone else in Oakdale with sneakers like mine," was all he said.

With that, he jogged ahead of Sam and Joe. Sam watched until he headed around a corner and out of sight.

"He's definitely up to something," Sam murmured. Every instinct in her body told her so! "And those sneaker prints behind the *Chronicle* office were his. I just know it."

"Which means he could be the thief," Joe said. He shook his head and kicked at the sidewalk. "Wow. That's pretty heavy-duty."

"Yeah, but we can't ignore the evidence." Sam bent to scratch Wishbone behind his ears, then looked up at Joe. "We should call David and tell him about Miss Gilmore's ring," she said. "Maybe he can meet us at my house for lunch. So much has happened so fast. Talking it out might help us get a handle on it all."

They used the phone at Pepper Pete's. Sam was glad when David said he could go to her house right away. After telling her father about Wanda's stolen ring, she and Joe headed out. Wishbone trotted along beside them.

"Great. He's here already," Sam said, as she and Joe turned onto her street a short while later. She waved and started jogging toward the house. "David, hi!"

He was bent close to the door. Hearing them, he turned around. As they came running up, he held out an envelope to Sam. "Hi, guys. This was wedged into the front door when I got here. There's no name on it."

Sam flipped the envelope over and opened it. Inside was a single folded sheet of white paper. Sam quickly unfolded it—and her breath caught in her throat.

In the center of the paper, five words had been spelled out using letters that had been clipped from a newspaper. Sam felt herself go ice-cold when she read the message:

CATCH ME IF YOU CAN.

"This must be from the thief!" Sam breathed. She held the note out so Joe and David could see it.

"'Catch me if you can,'" David read. "That's a definite challenge."

"Yeah. But why would the thief send it to you, Sam?" Joe asked.

Sam shivered. Why had the thief singled her out? It made her feel nervous—as if someone might be watching her even now. She quickly opened her front door and led the way inside.

"I don't know," she said. "It's as if the person is turning these thefts into something personal between the thief and me."

"Weird," David said.

Sam headed for the kitchen and took a can of tuna fish from the cupboard. "I'll say. I don't know why the thief picked me to challenge instead of someone else. But you know what?" She slapped the note down on the kitchen counter. "This just makes me more determined to catch whoever it is and get back the Civil

War medallion and Miss Gilmore's ring."

"So where do we start?" David asked.

"With the thefts," Sam answered right away. "Let's talk over everything we know about them. Maybe we'll see some kind of pattern."

A few minutes later, the kids were sitting around the kitchen table with tuna sandwiches and glasses of milk. Sam chuckled when she saw Wishbone circling around their feet, sniffing the air.

"Here you go, Wishbone," she said, tearing off a corner of her sandwich and feeding it to him. Then she turned back to Joe and David.

"Okay. We know the thief somehow managed to get in and out of the Kidds' house without Jimmy and me seeing," she began. She shook her head, letting out a long breath. "I still can't figure out how the person did it. There wasn't any way to get to the medallion without passing right by us!"

"The same thing was true at the *Chronicle*, right?" David asked.

Sam nodded. "Miss Gilmore locked the door when we left the office, and the only open window had security gates outside," she said. "When we got back, nothing had been disturbed."

"But the ruby ring was gone," Joe finished. He took a bite of his sandwich and washed it down with some milk.

"What you're saying is that the thief committed two impossible crimes," David said.

"Leaving hardly a clue," Joe added. "You said the police didn't find anything at the Kidds' house, right?"

"That's right," Sam confirmed. "But today, we did

find something—those muddy footprints behind the *Chronicle* office. And we know who made them."

David wasn't the kind of person who showed a lot of emotion. But Sam noticed his eyes widen when she told him about their encounter with Damont.

"You think he's the thief?" David asked.

"I don't want to think he is, but . . . well, the footprints point to him. And we was definitely acting suspicious," Sam said. "Plus, he knew about the medallion and Miss Gilmore's ruby ring."

"Definitely," Joe said. "He was with us at Pepper Pete's when Jimmy talked about his dad's Civil War medallion. And if he was lurking behind the *Chronicle* office, he would have heard Miss Gilmore talk about the ring." He reached under the table to feed the last bit of his sandwich to Wishbone. "Damont has to be our biggest suspect."

"But he's not the only one," David pointed out. "Everyone with us at Pepper Pete's yesterday knew about the Civil War medallion."

He was right, Sam realized. "And Isabel, Kayla, and I knew about Miss Gilmore's ring. That's a lot of suspects."

It was more than just the number of suspects that troubled her. "The worst thing is, they're all people we know," she went on. "Friends. I can't believe one of them could be a thief."

Even as she spoke, another thought occurred to Sam. "Unless we've got someone like A. J. Raffles on our hands," she added.

"The gentleman thief in *The Amateur Cracksman*?" Joe asked. "What made you think of him?"

"Well, Raffles has lots of friends," Sam explained. "But he's a thief, too."

Joe plunked his empty glass onto the table after finishing the last of his milk. "You said Raffles stole from the society types he's friends with, right?" he said.

Sam nodded. "There's this one story, called 'Gentlemen and Players.' I read it last night after you guys left," she said. "Raffles and Bunny are invited to this fancy country estate to play cricket. They pretend to be friends with the people."

"But they're really planning a heist?" David guessed.

"They've got their eye on an incredible diamond and sapphire necklace that belongs to one of the other guests," Sam said. "There's a detective from Scotland Yard at the estate. But Raffles manages to steal the necklace right out from under everyone's nose. And then he pretends to help look for the thief."

David stood up to take his empty plate to the sink. "Raffles sounds pretty daring."

"Just like the thief who's been striking around here," Sam said. She bit her lip, thinking about Damont. Did he have that kind of daring? She just couldn't make up her mind.

"It's hard to imagine," she said, "but I guess some people don't mind stealing from their friends."

Wishbone trotted through the doorway of Oakdale Attic Antiques ahead of Sam, Joe, and David later that afternoon. The bell hanging from the door jingled, and a round-faced, middle-aged man looked up from behind the counter with a pleasant smile.

"Hi there," the man greeted them. "I don't see you kids in here often. How can I help you?"

Wishbone sat down in front of the counter and smiled up at the man. "Hi, Phil. Tracking Dog and his pals are here on important detective work!"

"Hi, Mr. Hubbard," Sam said. "Actually, we wanted to ask you about jewelry."

Wishbone glanced around the store. There were several shelves along the walls, as well as some antique furniture and an umbrella stand. Among the items displayed Wishbone saw a stuffed owl, a wooden chest that smelled of must, and a velvet hat with a peacock feather jutting from it. Wishbone wagged his tail when he saw the earrings, watches, bracelets, and other jewelry on the shelves of the glass display counter behind which Phil stood.

"Looks as if we came to the right place!" he said to Sam, Joe, and David.

"I'll be glad to help you if I can," Phil said.

Wishbone sat back on his haunches and listened while his buddies told Phil about the stolen Civil War medallion and ruby ring. "I thought if we knew more about the things that were taken, that might give us a clue to who the thief is," Sam finished.

"Well . . ." Phil rubbed his chin thoughtfully. "Both of those pieces sound quite rare from the way you've described them. Possibly unique."

"So we're dealing with a thief who knows a lot about jewelry," David said.

"Definitely," Sam agreed. "The thief could have taken other stuff besides the medallion and the ruby ring. But nothing else was missing."

Phil nodded. "I'd say your thief is a person with very particular taste. Someone who goes for quality, not quantity."

Wishbone turned as the front door jingled. "Kayla?" he said.

The terrier crouched over his paws, watching carefully. Kayla still wore the embroidered shawl she'd thrown at Dinky earlier. Wishbone sought out Midnight with his eyes, ears, and nose. But this time the feline wasn't hidden beneath the folds of the shawl. All Wishbone saw were Kayla's black stretch pants and shiny blue tunic.

"Hi, Kayla." Sam turned to Kayla with a smile. "What are you doing here?"

"Shopping," Kayla said. "I want to get a gift to thank the St. Clairs for having me as a guest. Besides . . ." She grinned as she stepped over to the counter where the kids were talking to Phil. "I'm always game for something new. I thought I'd do some exploring while I'm in Oakdale."

"Where's Midnight?" David asked.

Wishbone watched as Kayla began browsing, picking things up off the shelves and examining them. She bent to inspect an unusual lacquered box that was displayed in one of the front picture windows. "He's napping," she said. "I guess all the excitement this morning wore him out."

Kayla's eyes flicked toward Wishbone. But the terrier's thoughts were focused on something she had just said. "Hmmm. If Midnight is napping, and you're here . . . that means his ball is up for grabs!"

"Isn't this a Chinese puzzle box?" Kayla asked, holding up the lacquered box she'd been looking at. "These are fabulous—filled with secret compartments. Opening them is quite a challenge, I've heard."

She took the box over to the counter, but Wishbone barely paid attention. He trotted over to the door and pawed at it. "Let the dog out, folks!"

Joe, Sam, and David were busy watching Kayla and Phil demonstrate how to move the different panels of the puzzle box to open it. None of them made a move in Wishbone's direction.

"This box is perfect. I'll take it," Kayla said, with a nod.

"And I'd like to leave, please!" Wishbone barked his request. "You see, Dinky and I have an appointment with a certain jingly ball. . . ."

It took only a moment for Phil to wrap the box and place it in a paper bag. Before he handed it over to Kayla, he reached through the open back of the display counter. "If you like unusual items, you might be interested in this bracelet, Miss Cooper," he said, pointing to something on the top shelf.

Wishbone sighed when he saw Kayla and the kids bend over the counter. "Don't forget about the dog, folks!" he barked.

"That's beautiful," Sam commented, watching Phil lift a bracelet of colorful stones from the shelf. "Check out the golden geometric designs linking the stones. They're really unusual."

"Those are Celtic designs," Phil said.

Wishbone saw Kayla's gaze rest on the bracelet for

a long moment. "It is lovely. But I'm afraid I can't buy it," she said. Raising an eyebrow, she waved toward the rest of the jewelry in the case. "I'd be careful if I were you, Mr. Hubbard. There's a thief on the loose, you know."

"And there's a dog on a mission!" Wishbone cried.

"Knowing about the thief does make me worry," Phil said, frowning. "I can't afford to—"

"Guys!" Sam said suddenly. Wishbone didn't miss the gleam of excitement in her eyes. "I just thought of a way to set a trap."

Wishbone pawed at the door yet again. "I'd say there's already a trap. It's keeping me from getting out!"

Sam and the others still didn't show any sign that they'd heard Wishbone. "Remember that sound monitor your parents used when Emily was a baby?" Sam said, turning toward David. "Do they still have it?"

Wishbone didn't hear David's answer. He heaved a happy bark as Kayla stepped toward the door.

"I'd say this gentleman has some business outdoors," Kayla said. She looked back over her shoulder at Joe. "I'm on my way. Shall I let him out?"

"You know the answer, Joe. Say yes!" Wishbone said to his best buddy.

Joe turned away from the others just long enough to nod. "Sure. Thanks, Kayla," he said.

As soon as Kayla pulled the door open, Wishbone sprinted onto the sidewalk.

"Freedom!" He kicked up his heels, racing in the direction of Dinky's house. "Look out, everyone! Tracking Dog is on his way!"

"This is our chance, Dinky." Wishbone trotted next to the Chihuahua on the grassy lawn behind Isabel's house. "All we have to do is find a way in and get Midnight's ball before he wakes up."

Dinky jumped up the wide stone stairs that led to the rear terrace. He paused on the top step and gazed at Wishbone.

"Good idea, Dinky. Let's try to get in this way." Wishbone moved quickly up the stairs and across the slate terrace to the French doors that led into the house. One look through the window panes, and he began to wag his tail. "There it is!"

The ball lay just a few feet inside the door. Sunlight glinted off its sparkly mirrors, and its satiny reds and blues. Looking at the ball, Wishbone could practically feel its rubber bumps in his teeth.

He made a quick survey of the room. "Hmm. There's Midnight. . . ." The Siamese lay curled up in the sunlight not far from the ball, fast asleep. "We're in luck, Dinky. There's an open window."

Wishbone trotted across the terrace and gazed up at the open window. Just beneath it, several potted plants sat on a table on the terrace. More plants were arranged at the foot of the table on the slate tiles.

"Excellent. We can climb up here, Dinky." Wishbone jumped onto the table, then waited for Dinky to join him. As soon as the Chihuahua clambered up next to him, Wishbone made his move. "Come on!"

He leaped through the open window and—

"What!" Mrs. St. Clair's shocked cry rang out in Wishbone's ears.

Wishbone and Dinky landed right in the woman's lap. Wishbone hadn't been able to see Isabel's mother from the French doors. But now he yelped as she sat bolt upright, swatting at him and Dinky with a magazine.

"Yikes! This calls for a slight change of plans, Dinky." Wishbone tried to dodge the magazine while he and Dinky clambered out of Mrs. St. Clair's lap. "Run!"

Chapter Nine

Wishbone scrambled off the couch, with Dinky right behind him.

"Get out of here, you two!" Mrs. St. Clair cried, shooing them away.

Wishbone ducked under Mrs. St. Clair's magazine. "I'd be glad to—just as soon as Dinky and I complete our mission." He raced toward the sunny spot where he'd seen Midnight's special ball—then stopped short.

Midnight was wide awake now. He sat in the sunshine next to the French doors, blinking innocently while he held his jingly ball in his teeth. He was so irritatingly calm. Wishbone couldn't resist trotting closer and barking. . . .

"What are those dogs doing in here!" a new voice boomed from behind him.

Looking over his haunches, Wishbone saw that it was Mrs. Hazlett, the housekeeper. The heavyset woman held a broom in her hand—and glowered at Wishbone and Dinky. "Out!" she cried.

"Uh-oh." Wishbone glanced nervously from Mrs. Hazlett to Isabel's mother. They were closing in on him and Dinky. "Like I said before, Dinky. Run!"

Wishbone leaped past Mrs. Hazlett's broom and scrambled through a doorway into the hall. He heard Dinky's claws clicking rapidly across the floor behind him—as well as the heavier treads of Mrs. Hazlett and Isabel's mother.

Wishbone had been to Isabel's house before. He knew the way to the front door. Moving as fast as his four legs would take him, he raced down the carpeted hallway. He barked when he caught sight of the carved wooden front door up ahead.

"There's the escape route. But how are we going to get the door open!" Wishbone leaped up at the doorknob. Dinky jumped too, but the little dog couldn't reach higher than Wishbone's haunches. Wishbone glanced behind him—and saw Mrs. Hazlett and Mrs. St. Clair.

"They're right behind us! We've got to—"

All of a sudden, Wishbone felt the carved door push inward. "What's going on?" a voice spoke up. Kayla's curious face appeared in the doorway, but Wishbone didn't stop to answer her question.

"Come on, Dinky," he barked out. "We are outta here!"

As he squeezed past Kayla through the doorway, Wishbone shot one last look inside. He saw Midnight, sitting calmly in the foyer, cleaning his whiskers with a silky black paw. In his green eyes was a look of clear victory.

"You haven't won this war yet. We'll be back!" Wishbone vowed.

He leaped onto the front yard. He glanced back to make sure Dinky was with him—then yelped when he saw the three women crowding through the front door. "Don't stop yet, Dinky!"

Wishbone skirted along the thick shrubs that lined the house. The cool, soft earth felt refreshing under his paws. When Dinky crouched to sniff beneath the bushes, Wishbone understood the lure. "This would be a perfect place to bury bones. But there's no time to stop, Dinky."

Dinky backed up, dragging a rolled-up newspaper out from beneath the bushes. The little dog could barely hold on to the bulky thing. But he kept dragging it, his tail wagging.

As Wishbone sniffed at the newspaper, his super-sensitive canine eyes picked out a distinctive pattern in the soft earth next to the newspaper.

"Hey! That's a sneaker print. And I've seen it before!" He crouched lower to sniff at the spot, then saw that there was a trail of the prints. "Whoever was behind the *Chronicle* office has been lurking around here, too!" A rustle in the shrubs somewhere nearby made Wishbone shoot forward. "And the person is still here!"

Running as fast as he could, Wishbone followed the trail through the shrubs. He could hear Dinky dragging the newspaper along behind him. From up ahead came the rustling of bushes. But the sound was growing fainter. When Wishbone rounded the corner of the house, the trail of sneaker prints ended at the grass. There wasn't a single person in sight.

"Hmm." Wishbone turned his head left and right,

panting. Whoever it was had gotten away.

Dinky's tail was still wagging as he dragged the newspaper up to Wishbone and dropped it. Taking the rolled-up thing in his muzzle, Wishbone trotted toward the street. "Maybe the pershon went thish way. . . ."

Dinky's legs moved quickly as he worked to keep up with Wishbone. As they neared the street, the little Chihuahua began running even faster. He raced across the street, letting out a stream of joyful barks.

Jimmy was sitting on his bike in his driveway. When he saw Dinky, the boy's face lit up. Jimmy grinned as the Chihuahua jumped around his legs. "Hi, boy!" he said.

"Shomeone left thish in the bushes!" Wishbone dropped the newspaper on the driveway and gazed expectantly at Jimmy. "Did you happen to see someone running away from Isabel's house just now?"

"You want to play, Wishbone?" Jimmy said. He picked up the newspaper and flung it into the air. "Okay, go get it!"

Wishbone sighed. "No one ever listens to the dog."

"Well, that about does it," Sam said. She gave a satisfied look around Oakdale Attic Antiques. "Our security system is in place."

She, Joe, David, and Phil Hubbard had been working for the past hour and a half. Sam was pleased with what they had come up with.

"This sound monitor is a truly inspired idea. Thanks for rigging it up, David," Phil said. He flipped the on switch of the monitor's small base unit, which sat on the counter next to the cash register. Then he picked up a smaller speaker component and made sure that it, too, was turned on. "All I have to do is carry this with me, and I'll hear everything that goes on in the store, right?"

David nodded. "I've enhanced the capabilities of the monitor so it can cover a larger area," he said. "As long as you're within two miles of the store, you'll hear every noise, Mr. Hubbard."

"If anyone tries to get in here, there should be lots of noise," Joe added.

He was standing on a ladder next to the front door, grinning down at them. Joe brushed his hand against a string of bells that he had just hung between the door and the doorframe. A loud jingling noise echoed through the store—and through the speaker of the sound monitor.

Phil shook his head, chuckling. "Those old sleigh bells have been collecting dust back in the storeroom for years. I sure am glad to put them to good use."

"We've strung bells across the front door and every single window," Sam said, as Joe climbed down from the ladder. "There's no way anyone could get in without setting them off."

Phil helped Joe fold the ladder. Then he carried it through a curtained doorway to a storage space at the back of the store. "I don't like knowing there's a thief around," he called out. "But I feel safer now."

When he reappeared a moment later, Phil was carrying his jacket. "I'd like to thank you three for helping me out," he said. "How about pizza?"

"Sounds great," Sam said.

The kids reached for their jackets, which were draped over the glass display counter next to the cash register. As Sam took hers from the pile, her eyes fell on a paper bag sitting on the floor. She caught a glimpse of black lacquer and tissue wrapping inside.

"Kayla forgot her Chinese puzzle box," she said. "I can bring it to her at the—"

A loud peal of bells rang out as the front door pushed open. Kayla held her hands over her ears, looking up at the bells in surprise. "I don't usually attract this much attention when I make an entrance," she joked.

"Like the security system?" Sam asked.

Kayla gave an impressed nod. "So this is the trap you were talking about," she said. "Very clever."

"It should give the thief a surprise," Joe added.

"Did you come back for this?" Sam asked, holding up the paper bag with the Chinese box in it.

Kayla let out a sigh of relief. She strode over to the counter and took the bag. "I got all the way back to the Ottingers' before I realized I'd forgotten it. I'm glad I made it back here before you closed the store, Mr. Hubbard."

"Sorry you had to make a special trip," Phil said. He put on his jacket and slipped the monitor's listening device into the pocket.

"I was planning to come back anyway. Isabel and I are meeting for pizza," Kayla said. "She and Midnight are waiting for me now at Pepper Pete's."

"We're headed there, too," David said.

The bells Joe had strung up jingled once more as

Phil opened the door to leave. Sam lingered behind to take one last look around the store. As her eyes flitted over the stuffed owl, the watches, and the gleaming gold of the Celtic bracelet Phil had shown them, one thought ran through her mind: *Please don't let the thief get anything else.*

She followed the others outside. There was another loud jingling as she closed the door. Even after Phil had locked it behind them, Sam could hear the bells through the speaker in his jacket.

Pepper Pete's was bustling when they got there. Isabel wasn't alone, Sam saw. Damont had taken a seat at her table, while Midnight batted his ball around on the floor beneath.

"What's with Damont?" Joe whispered in Sam's ear. "He was too busy to talk to us before. But now it looks as if he's got all the time in the world to hang out."

Sam noticed the way Damont watched Kayla as she sat down. Something in that look aroused Sam's distrust. "I'm going to keep an eye on him," she said.

Her dad was busy placing pepperoni rounds on an uncooked pizza shell. Sam took a moment to fill him in on all that had happened since she'd been in earlier. His face darkened when she told him about the note the thief had left her. But once he learned about the security plan they'd come up with for Oakdale Attic Antiques, he lightened up.

"Nice work, honey. With you on the case, this thief doesn't have much of a chance," he said.

The smile he shot at Sam was so full of confidence that Sam almost believed him. "Thanks, Dad," she told him. She glanced around the crowded restaurant, then grabbed an order pad from behind the counter. "Things are a little hectic. I'll take my table's order."

She saw that her group had pulled up chairs to sit with Kayla, Isabel, and Damont. Phil had placed the sound monitor on the table. As Sam picked out silverware and menus, the door opened and Jimmy Kidd walked in.

"Uh-oh," Sam murmured when she saw Dinky and Wishbone trot in behind him. She glanced nervously at Midnight. The cat paused with one black paw on his big jingly ball. "After what happened this morning . . ."

"Say no more." Kayla reached down, scooped up Midnight and his ball, and got to her feet. "This time it's your turn to go out, Midnight," she said, gently scratching the Siamese behind his ears. "It's only fair. Dinky and Wishbone were the ones who had to leave last time we were here."

As Kayla stepped past the dogs, Sam noticed the extra-alert way Wishbone and Dinky sniffed the air. But they seemed content to play with the newspaper Wishbone held in his muzzle.

"Where did you get that, boy?" Joe asked, pulling the newspaper free of Wishbone's muzzle.

"The *Star Reporter*, eh?" Kayla commented. She eyed the newspaper as she sat back down at the table. "Their reporters are always trying to get the scoop on me." She laughed down at Wishbone and Dinky. "Is that what all the commotion was about at the Ottingers' before?

Are you boys trying to get a story, too?"

"Commotion?" Joe echoed. "Did Wishbone cause some kind of trouble?"

"I'll say! He and Dinky practically gave my mother a heart attack," Isabel answered.

Sam was surprised to hear that Wishbone and Dinky had actually snuck inside Isabel's house and startled Mrs. St. Clair.

"I'm really sorry," Joe said.

"No harm done," Kayla told him, with an easy wave of her hand. "I've trained Midnight to handle himself. Now, let's see what news the *Star Reporter* is covering today. Alien abductions? Three-headed babies?"

Jimmy pointed to the newspaper as Joe spread it out on the table. "Hey, Damont. We brought back your newspaper," he said.

"What would I want with a gossip rag like the *Star Reporter*?" Damont scoffed. But Sam noticed that his cheeks turned slightly red.

Jimmy frowned. "You had it before, remember?" he insisted. "I saw it when you came past my house."

"It's not mine, Jimmy," Damont cut in. "Now drop it, okay?"

As Sam stared at Damont, her doubts about him bubbled to the surface again. Why didn't he want them to know the newspaper was his? What was he hiding? Did the *Star Reporter* have anything to do with the thefts?

Her gaze fell to Damont's backpack, which lay on the floor next to his chair. The zipper was only halfway shut. Through the gap, Sam caught sight of a second newspaper inside the pack.

Another *Star Reporter*? she wondered.

She bent closer—then did a double-take. It looked as if parts of the newspaper headlines had been cut out!

Suddenly, Damont's hand blocked Sam's view. He jerked the zipper all the way shut. When she looked up, the expression on his face was so dark that it made her shiver.

"Hey, look!" Joe's surprised voice made Sam look back at the table. He was pointing to the front page of the newspaper that Wishbone had brought in. "The front-page story. It's about you, Kayla!"

"And my parents," Isabel added, leaning across for a better look. "That must have been taken at that charity ball you went to a few months ago."

The photograph featured Kayla and Mr. and Mrs. St. Clair going into a building. Kayla and Isabel's mother both wore long, elegant dresses and gloves, but Sam barely noticed them. Her mind raced as she thought about Damont, the cut-up newspaper, and the note she'd received from the thief. . . .

"It's funny to see you so dressed up," David commented.

"People go all out for those events," Kayla said.

Sam shot another distracted glance at the photograph. In it, Isabel's mother was more dressed up than Sam had ever seen her in Oakdale. Large, teardrop-shaped diamonds hung from her necklace and bracelet. They sparkled so much that they practically jumped off the page at Sam.

She shook herself and turned to Damont. "I'm even more curious about something else," she said. "Like what you've got in—"

She broke off as she heard a metallic clinking sound from the monitor on the table. "Oh my gosh," she breathed. "The store!"

"That sounded like jewelry being moved!" Phil Hubbard reached for the monitor. Just as his fingers closed around it, a single word echoed from the speaker.

"Gotcha!"

Sam knew it could be only one person: *the thief*!

Chapter Ten

Wishbone had been sniffing at the basket of bread sticks on the table when he heard the low, gruff voice speak out from Phil's monitor. The very sound of it made the terrier's fur stand on end.

"Someone's in Attic Antiques!" he barked.

"It's the thief!" Phil cried, jumping to his feet. "I've got to get back to the store!"

All of a sudden there was an explosion of activity around Wishbone. "We're coming, too," Sam said, pushing back her chair.

Joe and David were already racing to the door. Wishbone joined them, scrambling through the gap as soon as Phil pushed the door open. As the others followed, Wishbone heard Sam's dad call out from behind the prep counter, "I'll call the police!"

"Follow Tracking Dog, people!" Wishbone heard pounding footsteps behind him as he raced around the corner of Oak Street toward Oakdale Attic Antiques. He picked up his speed when the store's double bay windows came into sight. "The thief won't get away with me on the trail!"

He leaped up, barking as he gazed through one of the bay windows.

"No one's there!" Phil said breathlessly, coming up behind Wishbone.

Wishbone scoured the store with his supersensitive canine eyes. Not a single person was in sight.

"The door's still locked," said Sam, watching as Phil twisted the knob and tried to pull.

"Someone's got to be in there. We all heard the voice on the monitor," David said.

Phil was already jabbing his key into the lock. He pushed the door open. Phil, Sam, Joe, David, and Wishbone raced inside amid a loud jingling of bells that made Wishbone shake his ears.

"Excellent security system!" Wishbone gazed up at the string of bells hanging from the door. "But where's the thief?"

Phil's face was tight as he ran through the curtained doorway to the back storeroom. Wishbone crouched down, ready to leap at any intruder. But when Phil returned a moment later, he was alone. "It's empty," he said, a look of total confusion on his face. "Whoever was here is gone."

Wishbone heard Sam gasp. She gaped at the glass display counter where the sound monitor and the cash register were. "I think something else is gone, too," she breathed. "Mr. Hubbard, you'd better come over here."

Phil was next to her in a flash. "The Celtic bracelet," he said, staring in horror at the top display shelf. "The thief got it!"

"But how?" Joe shoved his hands in the pockets of his basketball jacket. "Not a single bell sounded before we came in. The door was locked. . . ."

Seeing a police squad car pull up in front of the store, Wishbone trotted over to the door. "The thief has struck again, Officer Krulla!" he said as the husky officer came in.

"The thief did it again, Officer Krulla," Sam said. "A Celtic bracelet was just stolen from the store."

Wishbone sighed. "Didn't I just say that?"

The officer's eyes flitted quickly over the store. "Your father called in, Sam. Said something about trapping the thief?"

Wishbone sat back on his haunches while his friends told Officer Krulla about the long-range monitor and the bells they had set up. "Not that it did any good," Phil finished, nodding toward the bells that hung from the door. "The thief got in and out without sounding the alarm."

"Is there any other way in or out?" Officer Krulla asked.

"A window in the storeroom," Phil told him. "I had security bars installed over it a few years back."

Wishbone trotted through the curtained doorway behind the two men. Old clothing and furniture were piled around the room. The dusty smell of it made Wishbone's nose itch. He was glad for the fresh air that came in through the open window at the back of the room.

"That window never has shut properly, but . . ." Phil gave a nod as Officer Krulla reached through and tested the bars. "See? They haven't been disturbed. Even if they had been, the bells we strung up here would have rung out."

Phil ran a finger across the bells. "To tell you the truth, I don't know how the thief managed it," he said, speaking above the loud, jingling noise. "It was impossible for anyone to get in."

Officer Krulla pulled his police notebook from his back pocket and flipped it open. He tapped it thoughtfully with his pen as he and Phil went back into the main room of the store, with Wishbone trotting alongside. "You say a Celtic bracelet was stolen?" he asked.

"That's right," Phil told him. "I acquired it at an auction recently. Whoever took the bracelet knows about jewelry. To look at it, you would never know the bracelet was so special. But it was by far the rarest piece in my store."

"Just like Miss Gilmore's ring and Mr. Kidd's medallion," Sam pointed out. "They were unique, too."

Officer Krulla made a few quick notes in his book. "Clearly, the thief is after only the most valuable and rare items," he said.

"And now that the dust is out of my nose, Tracking Dog is after the thief!" Wishbone put his nose to the ground and started sniffing. He moved to the glass counter where the bracelet had been displayed. A thick pane of glass covered the front of the counter. But Wishbone sniffed around at the back, which was open.

"Mmmm. That leather watchband would smell even better after a few days in Wanda's flower beds." Wishbone paused as he caught sight of a small black box taped to the underside of the glass counter, just beneath the cash register. "What's this?"

He rose up on his hind paws and sniffed at the plastic box. A faint humming sound came from it. Through a small window at the front of the box, Wishbone could see a tape winding slowly from one sprocket to another.

"A tape player!" Wishbone looked back over his haunches and barked to the others. "I've found something, everyone. Hellllooo!"

Another impossible theft, thought Sam. How could this have happened?

She'd been fighting back her frustration, trying to listen to Phil describe the Celtic bracelet to Officer

Krulla. But Wishbone's sudden barking made it impossible to hear what was said. Looking over, Sam saw that the terrier was on his hind legs, sniffing at something in the glass display counter.

"Leave that alone, Wishbone," Phil said, frowning.

"I think he's trying to show us something, Mr. Hubbard," Joe said. He jogged over to the display counter and bent down to look underneath the top shelf. "Whoa," he said, letting out a low whistle. "There's a tape recorder under here!"

Sam leaped forward. "That's definitely not part of our security system," she said.

She held her breath as Officer Krulla reached beneath the counter. A moment later he held up a small, black portable tape player. "Does this belong to you, Phil?" he asked, as he pulled off the tape.

Phil shook his head. "Someone else must have put it there," he said. "But why?"

"I bet the thief left it there!" Sam said, feeling a new rush of excitement. "Let's listen to it."

Officer Krulla rewound the tape, then hit the PLAY button. Sam listened, but all she heard was recorded silence. They let the tape player run for several minutes. But still . . .

"Nothing," David said. "I don't get it. Why would someone go to the trouble of putting that there when there's nothing—"

He was interrupted by a single word that suddenly sounded from the tape player: "Gotcha!"

"That's what we heard in Pepper Pete's," Sam realized. "The voice was taped!"

"I understand." David leaned against the counter, crossing his arms over his chest. "The thief must have timed the recording to play after he or she made away with the bracelet. That's why there was all that silence at the beginning of the tape. It gave the thief time to get away before we knew anything had happened."

"The voice was low, and pretty gruff," Sam said, knitting her brow in concentration. "It sounded like a guy, but . . . I don't know. I guess a girl could disguise her voice to sound like that, too."

She stopped herself from asking the question that popped into her head: Was it Damont? It sounded kind of like him, but she couldn't be sure.

As she went over the crime in her head, Sam felt more and more frustrated. "How did the thief get in and out without triggering the alarm we set up?" she wondered out loud. "Who is it?"

"Beats me," David said. "But I think we have to rule out our biggest suspect. Damont was with us at Pepper Pete's when the bracelet was taken."

He was right, Sam realized. That meant they were back at square one. "This is no ordinary thief, guys. This is someone who can accomplish the impossible," she said.

"Someone who likes to brag about it, too," Joe added. "That recording was the thief's way of making sure we know our security system isn't good enough to stop a really great thief."

"A master," Sam agreed. "Just like A. J. Raffles."

Phil raised an eyebrow. "Who?"

Sam told him and Officer Krulla about Raffles and

Bunny, the gentlemen thieves in E. W. Hornung's stories. "Raffles loves the challenge of the most impossible crimes," she explained. "And the game of playing the perfect gentleman when he's actually a cunning thief. I guess he's kind of vain, too."

"What do you mean?" Joe asked.

"Well . . ." Sam twisted the ends of her blond hair while she thought it out. "Even though he doesn't want to be found out, Raffles can't stand the idea of anyone else taking credit for his brilliant crimes. That's what happens in a story I started reading last night, 'To Catch a Thief.'"

"How many stories did you read last night, anyway?" David asked, arching an eyebrow at her.

"Just three," Sam said, laughing. "What can I say? Being suspected of stealing made it hard to go to sleep. Anyway, in the story, Raffles gets really mad when he finds out another thief is imitating his and Bunny's style."

"You mean, stealing from England's high society?" David asked.

Sam nodded. "Yes. So Raffles and Bunny decide to catch the person by using their own criminal logic to figure out the thief's next move," she went on.

"Um, Sam? This is interesting, but . . ." Phil Hubbard frowned, tapping the compact tape player Officer Krulla had placed on the counter. "What does it have to do with getting my Celtic bracelet back?"

Sam laid her hand on the counter in a determined fist. "I think we can do the same thing to catch the thief right here in Oakdale," she said.

Seeing the blank faces staring back at her, she went on, "All we have to do is start thinking like our thief, trying to anticipate what the person might do next. I know we can catch whoever it is. We just have to keep in mind what Raffles says . . ." Sam grinned, shooting a challenging look around the room. "'It takes a thief to catch a thief.'"

Chapter Eleven

Wishbone chased the dried leaves on the sidewalk as he trotted out of Oakdale Attic Antiques ahead of his friends a half hour later. "So . . . it takes a thief to catch a thief." Kicking up his heels, he ran back to Joe and jumped around his feet. "This sounds like a job for Tracking Dog! Dinky and I have been planning a heist of our own!"

He gazed up at his best buddy. Joe looked preoccupied as he walked. "Three things have been stolen," Joe said, "and Officer Krulla still doesn't seem to have a clue to who the thief is."

"That's because he's thinking like a police officer," Sam said, "instead of like—"

"A thief," David finished. "I bet you're right, Sam. We might have better luck tracking down the culprit if we try to put ourselves in the thief's shoes."

"Sounds good to me. But there's something I need to do first, guys," Joe said.

Wishbone didn't like the serious way his best buddy

was looking at him. "It's not time for my shots, is it?"

"It sounded as if Wishbone and Dinky sent out some pretty serious shock waves at Isabel's house before," Joe went on. "I want to head over there and talk to Mrs. St. Clair. You know, to make sure everything is okay."

"Dinky and I are not the bad guys here, Joe. We were on a mission!" Wishbone protested. Thinking about Midnight's colorful ball with nubs and satiny soft spots made him wag his tail faster. "Then again, a trip to Isabel's would mean another chance to snag that ball." The terrier trotted ahead more quickly. "Let's go!"

"Why don't we go, too?" Sam suggested.

"So we can put our heads together and start thinking like thieves?" David said. "Sounds good to me."

He laughed, but Wishbone saw that Sam's face remained serious. "You know," she said slowly, "there's something about what just happened that bothers me."

"Three valuable pieces of jewelry are missing." Joe kicked at the sidewalk with his sneaker. "That would bother anyone."

Sam nodded thoughtfully. "I know, but I still feel that we're missing some important clue."

"You mean about Damont?" Joe suggested. "That the voice on the tape sounded kind of like his."

"You noticed that too, huh?" Sam said. "But Damont was with us at Pepper Pete's, remember? He couldn't have taken the bracelet." She knit her brow into a dark frown as she added, "Still, the sneaker prints, the newspaper . . . they both point to him."

"The newspaper?" David shoved his hands in his pockets and shot a questioning glance at Sam. "What are you talking about?"

Wishbone's ears perked up when Sam told them about seeing a second newspaper in Damont's backpack.

"I didn't get a close look," Sam said, "but I was sure some of the letters had been cut out of the headlines."

"So Damont could be the person who sent you that note!" Joe's whole face lit up. But then he frowned and said, "But we already decided he couldn't be the thief, since he was at Pepper Pete's when the bracelet was stolen."

"That's exactly what's bothering me." Sam sighed, kicking at a tuft of grass at the edge of the sidewalk. "We're out of suspects, guys."

Before long, Wishbone trotted ahead of his friends up the curved drive toward Isabel's big stone house. He wagged his tail, looking in all directions for Midnight's ball. He didn't spot it. But a rustling sound in the bushes next to the house caught his ear. Whipping his head around, he spotted a dark head crouched just beneath one of the arched windows.

"Someone's there!" he alerted his friends. Letting out a loud stream of barks, he raced toward the spot.

"Someone's lurking in the bushes next to Isabel's!" Joe said.

Wishbone heard a gasp from the bushes and saw two eyes focus on him. As the figure jumped back from the window and started to run, Wishbone saw the tall build of a boy.

"He's running!" Sam cried. She started after the

person, but Wishbone was way ahead of her.

"Tracking Dog's not going to let him get away this time!" Wishbone's paws thudded on the grass as he loped closer. He made a final leap, cutting off the person before he reached the corner of the house.

"Hey!" The boy stopped short, panting, and Wishbone got a clear look at his face.

"Damont!" Sam cried as she raced up. David and Joe were right behind her. "What are you doing here?"

Damont's eyes flitted wildly around. Wishbone had the impression he might try to make a break for it. Jumping around the boy's feet, Wishbone barked out, "Don't even think about it!"

"First we find you sneaking around outside the *Chronicle* building right when Miss Gilmore's ruby ring was stolen," Joe said, facing Damont. "And now this."

"What are you going to do? Have me arrested for hanging around with dangerous shrubbery?" Damont said sarcastically. "You guys don't know what you're talking about!"

"Oh, yeah?" Sam crossed her arms over her chest. "Then I'm sure you won't mind if I take a look at the newspaper in your pack," she said. "The one with the letters cut out of it? I'm sure the police will be very interested when they see that the cutouts match the letters on a note that the thief left me."

Damont's smug expression faded. "Letter? I didn't write any letter!"

"Then you won't have any problem letting us look in your pack," Sam shot back smoothly. "Or explaining the newspaper to Officer Krulla."

Damont raked a hand through his hair. He looked from Sam to his pack, and then let out his breath in a rush. "I don't know how that newspaper got in my pack. I'm not a thief!"

Wishbone knew that Damont wasn't above telling a white lie now and again. But this time, his canine instincts told him the boy was telling the truth.

"Prove it," Joe challenged.

"Okay, okay. I'll tell you what my project is," Damont finally said. "Not that it's any of your business, but I've been trying to get a photograph of Kayla for the *Star Reporter*."

"The *Star Reporter*?" David echoed. "Why?"

"Hey. Kayla's big news, and suddenly she shows up right here in Oakdale." Damont gave a smug smile and gestured toward Isabel's house. "I figured the *Star Reporter* would pay big bucks for an exclusive shot. Why shouldn't I be the person to get it?"

Wishbone sniffed at Damont's hands. "How about an exclusive shot of the Tracking Dog? I'll have you know we canines are very photogenic."

"Is that why you were lurking around behind the *Chronicle* building this morning?" Sam asked. "You were trying to get a photo of Kayla?"

Damont nodded. "You got it, Sherlock," he said. "Too bad I couldn't get a good view of her, with you and Isabel and Miss Gilmore all crowding around." He frowned around at Sam. "Actually, it seems like someone is always in the way. Last night it was you and Jimmy, Sam. I was cutting across Jimmy's yard when I saw you going to the shed."

Wishbone heard Sam draw in her breath sharply. "You mean you're the one who locked us in there?" she asked.

"Jimmy's always following me around. I didn't want him interfering with my shot," Damont explained.

"So you scared your own cousin half to death just to make some money?" Sam said. "How can you be sure the *Star Reporter* would even pay for a photo of Kayla?""I called them," Damont answered. Wishbone noticed that he didn't seem the least bit sorry for the trouble he had caused. "I was talking to someone from their office this morning when your dog started bothering me, Talbot."

Wishbone gave an indignant bark. "Hey! Tracking Dog was performing important detective work."

"So are you telling us you didn't make the recording

that we found at Oakdale Attic Antiques?" Sam asked.

Damont looked at her blankly. "What are you talking about?"

"What about the letter I got from the thief?" Sam persisted. "Can I see the newspaper in your pack?"

Wishbone saw a glimmer of uncertainty flicker in Damont's eyes. He unzipped his pack and pulled out the newspaper. As Sam took it, Wishbone sniffed at the irregular shapes that had been cut from the newsprint.

"Someone else must have put that in my pack," Damont said. "The first time I noticed it was when I saw you staring into my pack at Pepper Pete's."

"We're supposed to believe that?" Joe asked, shooting a dubious glance at Damont.

"Believe whatever you want, Talbot," Damont muttered.

Wishbone watched the boy closely. His canine senses didn't pick up any deceit. "It's the truth, Joe," he said, licking his buddy's hand.

Damont pulled a camera from the pocket of his jacket and shoved it into his backpack. "At this rate, I'll never get a photo of Kayla," he said. "Somehow she always manages to keep me from getting a clear shot."

"You sound as if she knows you're there," Sam said. She spoke lightly, but Wishbone noticed that Damont's expression only darkened.

"That's what it feels like. Kayla's never said anything to me, but . . . it's as if she's doing everything she can to keep me from getting a good shot." Damont frowned, gazing back at Isabel's house. Then he shook himself and said, "Never mind. That's impossible, right?"

Chapter Twelve

Sam stretched out in her bed on Sunday morning and glanced at the clock on her bedside table. Eight-thirty. Still plenty of time before she had to get ready to go to Pepper Pete's with her dad. The pizzeria didn't open until eleven.

Which means I can finish reading "To Catch a Thief," Sam thought.

She punched up her pillows, leaned against them with her copy of *The Amateur Cracksman,* and flipped it open to the page she had marked. As she began to read, Sam felt herself transported to London just before the turn of the century—with its foggy nights, gas-lit lamps, and horse-drawn hansom cabs. She could easily picture Raffles and Bunny in their elegant suits as they planned to outsmart the thief who was imitating them.

The more Sam read about Raffles, the more impressed she was with his shrewd intelligence. He had identified the culprit by a process of elimination, comparing the names of the people who had been present at all the thefts. One name kept reappearing—that of Lord Belville, a man who no longer had the fortune to support his high-society lifestyle. Raffles decided to outwit Belville by waiting for him to return to his home with some newly stolen loot—and then taking it from him.

Sam found herself rooting for Raffles and Bunny, hoping they would catch the copycat thief and get his stolen loot. While they waited, they looked everywhere for Belville's cache of stolen jewels. But for once, success seemed to elude the gentleman thief. Raffles became so frustrated that he and Bunny started to argue. Sam held her breath as Raffles grabbed a pair of wooden Indian clubs, which he swung to threaten his partner.

Then suddenly everything changed. Sam whistled under her breath as Raffles made the important discovery: one of the clubs was hollow. Inside were the jewels he and Bunny had been searching for. In the end, not only did Raffles catch the thief, but he found all the jewels Lord Belville had stolen.

Raffles is a master, no doubt about it, Sam thought. *Even the best imitator is no match for him.*

She was still thinking about A. J. Raffles—and Oakdale's thief—as she got dressed and went into the kitchen.

"Hi, honey." Her father glanced up from his coffee and newspaper with a smile. "You look serious this morning," he said. "Something on your mind?"

"Guilty," Sam said. She headed for the refrigerator and poured herself a glass of orange juice. "I was thinking about the thefts. I just have this feeling that the way to catch the thief is to beat the person at his or her own game. But . . ." She reached for some cereal and a bowl, trying to put her thoughts into words. "Well, A. J. Raffles could think like a thief because he *was* one. It's fun to think about acting like that, but I don't know if I feel comfortable actually doing it."

"Being tricky and underhanded isn't exactly your style, Sam," her dad pointed out.

"Tell me about it." Sam poured milk on her cereal and joined him at the table. "I like things to be clear and straightforward," she said. "But that approach definitely isn't going to work with whoever's been stealing stuff around Oakdale. The thief is too crafty."

Her father folded his newspaper and leveled a long, thoughtful look at her. "You're a smart kid, Sam," he said. "I know you'll do the right thing."

"I hope so," Sam said, wishing she felt half as sure as he did. "Anyway, Joe and David are going to meet me at Pepper Pete's this morning to try to figure out what our next step should be."

Wishbone began wagging his tail as he followed Joe into Pepper Pete's on Sunday morning. The scents of garlic, tomatoes, and pepperoni floated temptingly on the air. To Wishbone, it smelled like heaven.

"Hi, Sam!" The terrier trotted over to the prep counter, where Sam was busy filling shakers with garlic salt and hot pepper. Sam's dad stood behind the counter, tossing pizza dough. "Hi, Walter! The sauce smells extra-tasty today," Wishbone said, rising up on his hind legs.

He saw that David was there, too, stacking pizza boxes at the far end of the counter. Wishbone sat back on his haunches and gazed up at the boy. "Tracking Dog would be glad to help you with that—for a small, edible reward."

"Thanks for coming, guys," Sam said. She reached down to scratch Wishbone behind his ears, then laughed when she saw him sniff the air. "Don't tell me you're hungry already, Wishbone. Okay, boy. Here you go."

Wishbone's mouth was open and ready for the bread stick she dropped into it.

"Why don't you take a break?" Sam's father suggested, as Wishbone crunched down on the crisp bread stick.

"But I just got started!" Wishbone objected. Then he realized that Walter wasn't even looking at him. "Oh, you mean Sam. I knew that."

Walter poured three glasses of soda from the fountain and set them down on a tray. "We don't have any customers yet."

"Sounds good, Dad. We can talk over there, guys." Sam wiped her hands on her white apron, then grabbed the tray and headed for one of the booths next to the windows.

"Thanks for the sodas, Mr. Kepler," David said. He slid into the booth next to Sam, while Joe sat across from them. "So where do we start?" David asked.

Wishbone saw the determined set to Sam's face as he jumped up next to Joe. "I want to try something Raffles and Bunny did in 'To Catch a Thief,'" she said.

Just hearing Sam mention E. W. Hornung's stories made Wishbone wag his tail faster. They were filled with such atmosphere and adventure! Wishbone perked up his ears, listening intently while Sam described how Raffles and Bunny had identified the thief who was copying them.

"So . . ." Joe said, poking at his soda with his straw, "when Raffles compared who was present at each of the crimes, he figured out who the thief was?"

Sam nodded.

"You think we should try the same thing, huh?" David smoothed out his napkin and took a pen that Sam pulled from her apron pocket. "Let's start with the Kidds' gold medallion. Who had access to the Kidds' house or knew about the medallion?"

"I definitely go on that list," Sam said. "Plus Jimmy."

"And Damont," Joe added. "He's the one who locked you guys in the shed, remember?"

David nodded, writing down the names. "I'm adding everyone who was at Pepper Pete's when Jimmy talked about the medallion, too," he said. "Joe, Isabel, Mr. and Mrs. St. Clair, and Kayla. I think that's it. Now, what about the ruby ring that was taken from the *Chronicle* office?"

Wishbone sniffed at the paper napkin as David started a second list.

"Well, Wanda, Kayla, Isabel, and I all saw the ring," Sam said, counting off the names on her fingers. "And we know Damont was lurking around near the windows, trying to get a photograph of Kayla. So he probably knew about it, too."

Joe took a drink of his soda, staring down at the names. "So far, Sam, Kayla, Isabel, and Damont knew about both the medallion and the ruby ring."

Wishbone saw the frown that settled over Sam's face. "That's a pretty big list. Can't we narrow it down?" she said. "I mean, not many people knew about the Celtic bracelet at Oakdale Attic Antiques."

"Or about our security system," David added. "The thief definitely knew about it, or we wouldn't have found that recorded message."

He leaned forward, mumbling names as he wrote them on a third list on the napkin. "There's the three of us, and Mr. Hubbard. We all knew about the bracelet and the security system."

"Don't forget about Kayla. She saw the security system," Sam said.

"And me!" Wishbone barked across the booth. But his friends were so busy looking at the lists, they didn't seem to notice. Wishbone gazed at the lists on the napkin:

KIDDS' HOUSE	CHRONICLE	OAKDALE ATTIC ANTIQUES
Sam	Wanda	Sam
Jimmy	Kayla	Joe
Damont	Isabel	David
Joe	Sam	Mr. Hubbard
Isabel	Damont	Kayla
Mr. St. Clair		
Mrs. St. Clair		
Kayla		
David		

David went down the three lists, making check marks on any name that was repeated. "I think we can rule out Sam as a suspect," he said, crossing out her name. "That leaves . . ." He straightened up suddenly, jabbing his pen at the paper. "Guys! There's just one person who knew about all three stolen pieces!"

"Who? Who? Who?" Wishbone turned questioning eyes toward each of his friends. "Talk to the dog, folks!"

Sam bent over the napkin, then did a double-take. "Whoa," she breathed. "It's Kayla!"

Sam couldn't stop staring at Kayla's name. It was on all three lists. With a check mark next to each. Why hadn't she seen it before?

"Kayla's the thief," she said. "She's got to be."

"No way," Joe spoke up right away. "She was bike riding with Isabel when the Kidds' medallion was stolen. And she was with you when the thief took Miss Gilmore's ring."

"Not to mention that she's been trying to help us catch the thief," David pointed out. He drank up the last of his soda, then stirred the ice cubes with his straw. "It couldn't be Kayla."

Still, Sam's gut instincts told her they'd found the culprit. Her whole body buzzed with excitement as she tried to fit all the pieces together. "Raffles did that kind of stuff all the time. He came up with alibis or pretended to search for a thief when he himself had committed the crime," she explained. "It was part of the game he played.

"Remember when Jimmy talked about the Civil

War medallion?" she went on. The words tumbled from her mouth like water rushing over a streambed. "Kayla definitely acted interested. She took a pretty close look at Miss Gilmore's ring, too. And at the Celtic bracelet." Sam leaned forward, brushing her blond hair from her face. "I bet anything she left the Chinese puzzle box in the store on purpose after she heard us talking about setting a trap. That way she had an excuse to come back later to see what we had done. And I bet that's when she planted the tape recorder under the counter!"

David just shook his head. "I don't think so, Sam. She was with us when the bracelet was taken, remember? Besides, her family is so famous. They must have tons of money."

It was a logical response. But Sam knew logic wasn't enough to beat this thief. "Kayla's always talking about what a game life is, how the world is a playground," she said. "I mean, think about the note the thief left for me, and that recording she planted at Oakdale Attic Antiques. . . . She even gave me this copy of *The Amateur Cracksman*."

Sam pulled the book from the pocket of her apron and slapped it down on the table. She'd brought it to read when the restaurant was slow. But now she looked at it in a whole new light. "It's as if Kayla was giving me a hint, or making a challenge or something."

"You think this whole thing is some kind of game to her? Stealing valuable jewelry from people who never did anything to her?" Joe crunched down on some ice cubes from his soda glass, shaking his head. "It doesn't make sense."

"Even if it did," David added, "we still don't have any proof that Kayla's the thief. How did she get in and out of any of the places where things were taken? It's impossible."

That was the hard part, thought Sam—coming up with concrete evidence. "Kayla didn't leave anything to go on," she admitted. "Still, I know she's the thief."

She drummed her fingers against the tabletop, gazing distractedly out the window. She could see Kilgore Gurney through the upstairs window of his used-book shop, Rosie's Rendezvous Books, across the street. Travis Del Rio was rolling a rack of sale items out onto the sidewalk in front of Oakdale Sports & Games. Sam watched distractedly as people ambled toward the Dart Animal Clinic and Snooks Furniture. Any one of them could be Kayla's next target, she thought.

"That's it!" she cried, sitting bolt upright.

Joe and David both stared at her blankly. Even Wishbone seemed to be watching her with eyes that begged for an explanation.

"I'll bet anything that Kayla's crime spree isn't over yet," Sam told them. "We just have to figure out what her next step will be and then set a trap so we can catch her in the act!"

"If she's the thief. We still don't know that for sure," Joe reminded her.

Sam's thoughts were racing. "In 'To Catch a Thief,' Raffles and Bunny set a trap for Lord Belville," she said. "Raffles guessed what Belville's next heist would be. Then he and Bunny waited in Belville's apartment to catch him red-handed when he returned with the loot."

"'It takes a thief to catch a thief.'" David's face was thoughtful as he reached for Sam's copy of *The Amateur Cracksman*. "So the big question is, when and where will Oakdale's thief strike next?"

As he flipped through the pages, Sam's gaze fell on the card she'd been using as a bookmark. "What about the party Isabel's family is throwing for Kayla?" she asked. She plucked the card from between the pages and held it up. "That's got to be when she's going to strike next."

The realization hit her like a bolt of lightning. But Joe didn't seem nearly as convinced. "Do you really think Kayla would steal something at a party that's being thrown by family friends? In her honor?" he asked.

"I know it sounds weird," Sam admitted. "But I think a party like that is an opportunity the thief won't pass up. Especially if anyone there has rare jewels. Just yesterday Isabel said something about her family having lots of valuable jewelry."

"Remember that photo of Isabel's mom? The one in the *Star Reporter*? You guys saw that diamond necklace and bracelet she was wearing." David glanced back and forth between his two friends. "They looked as if they were worth plenty."

"David, you're a genius!" Sam crowed. "That's what Kayla's going to steal. Think about it. The diamond necklace and bracelet are rare and valuable—just like the other things the thief has been going after. And taking something we've all gotten a look at—that's exactly the kind of game the thief has been playing with us."

"Yeah," Joe said slowly. "But I just can't see Kayla stealing from good friends. I'm still not convinced she's the person we're after."

"We'll find out for sure tonight at the reception," Sam said, with a firm nod. She gazed down at the invitation, her heart beating a mile a minute. "This time, we're going to catch the thief in the act."

Chapter Fourteen

Fifteen minutes later, Sam hung up the telephone in the rear hallway of Pepper Pete's. She let out a long breath. After being stumped by the thief for so long, she felt as if they were finally on the right trail. She just hoped their plan worked!

When she got back to the main part of the restaurant, Joe and David both looked up expectantly from their booth. Wishbone had jumped down from the bench. He was sniffing around the feet of three teenage boys who had just walked in the door.

"Did you talk to Isabel?" Joe asked.

"Yes. And to her parents." Sam placed menus on the table where the teenagers were sitting down. Then she leaned into her friends' booth and said in a low voice, "It was kind of tricky. I mean, I didn't say anything about Kayla being our top suspect. I just said we thought the thief might strike during their party, and that we have a plan to try to catch the person."

"And?" David prompted.

Sam readjusted her apron, placing her pen and

order pad in the pocket. "Mr. and Mrs. St. Clair totally agreed when I told them I thought the plan should be secret. They said they wouldn't tell anyone, not even Kayla," she said. "I guess they want to do everything they can to protect their diamond jewelry, even if it means keeping a secret from a close family friend."

"What if Kayla overheard them talking to you?" Joe asked, frowning. "She *is* staying in their house."

"Kayla wasn't home when I called. Isabel told me she's out taking a walk with Midnight." Sam couldn't hide her excitement as she added, "She told me something else, too. Kayla isn't as rich as we thought."

Joe arched a dark eyebrow at her. "She's not?"

Sam shook her head. "Her parents give her an allowance. Isabel says it's the Coopers' way of teaching Kayla to be responsible with money. I guess Kayla spent all her allowance during her trip to India and Nepal. So now she's got to earn her own money until the end of the year. Isabel told me that's when Kayla gets next year's allowance."

"Wow." David said. He and Joe exchanged sober glances across the table. "That's a motive, all right."

Sam looked over her shoulder at the table of older boys. "Let me just take this order," she said. "Then we can go over exactly what we're going to do at Kayla's party tonight."

"So many yummy smells!" Wishbone wagged his tail and sniffed the air early Sunday evening. "Let me see: cheese, pastry puffs, and . . . yes! Delectable pigs-in-blankets. My favorites!"

The food had been calling to him ever since he and his friends had arrived at Isabel's house a short while earlier. The mouth-watering scents drew him down the hall toward the living room. But as Wishbone passed the half-open door to the library, he remembered that his reason for being at Isabel's had nothing to do with food.

Eating will have to wait, he reminded himself. Tracking Dog has more important work to do!

Wishbone trotted through the doorway and onto the thick Oriental carpet that covered the library floor. Sam, Joe, and David were clustered around a closet set into the side wall, along with Isabel and her father. As soon as Wishbone saw them, he felt it. A sense of excitement that made him want to kick up his hind paws and race around the room.

"Tracking Dog is ready for action," Wishbone reported. "I'll guard the scene while you set the trap!" He stood at the open doorway and glanced up and down the hall. "So far the suspect is nowhere in sight."

"There," Mr. St. Clair's voice came from behind the terrier. "I've placed our most valuable jewelry in the safe," he said.

Glancing back over his haunches, Wishbone saw Isabel's dad step back and brush his hands together. Beyond him, inside the closet, a squat, sturdy-looking metal safe stood on the floor. David was hunched over it. On his face was the kind of intense concentration Wishbone usually exhibited while gnawing on Ellen's tastiest soup bones.

"We haven't felt the need to use this safe in a long time," Mr. St. Clair said. "I can't believe we don't even know the combination."

"Don't worry—the electronic alarm is all set up," David assured him. "We'll just close the safe door without locking it." He stood up and stepped out of the closet with a smile. "If anyone tampers with the safe, the alarm will go off. It's almost as good as having a locked safe."

"Excellent work!" Wishbone barked his approval, wagging his tail.

He watched carefully while Mr. St. Clair locked the closet and slipped the key in his pants pocket. "Can't hurt to lock at least one door," he said.

"Okay," Sam said, taking a deep breath. "Does

everyone remember what to do?"

Joe nodded. "David and I stake out the hallway."

"I'll be keeping an eye on everyone in the living room," Isabel added.

"And I'll be standing right here," Sam said, planting herself firmly outside the closet door.

"What about Wishbone?" Isabel asked. She bent down and petted the short, soft fur of his muzzle.

"You be sure to stay out of trouble, boy," Joe said. He crouched down so that he was nose-to-nose with Wishbone. "We don't want anything to wreck our plan."

Wishbone wagged his tail and smiled up at his best buddy. "Don't worry, Tracking Dog will be making the rounds, too!" he promised.

Sam looked curiously toward the hallway, then lowered her voice and said, "You're sure no one except us knows about the plan?"

"Definitely," Isabel told her. "Kayla and my mom have been upstairs getting ready. Mom asked Kayla to help her so that we could set up our trap without even Kayla knowing."

Wishbone perked up his ears at the sound of the doorbell. He could feel the charged excitement that shot through the room.

"This is it!" Sam said, crossing her fingers.

Wishbone trotted out of the library in time to see Isabel's mother come sweeping down the wide stairs to the foyer in a black cocktail dress. Wishbone gave her a big smile. "Hi, Mrs. St. Clair! No need to worry. Tracking Dog is officially on duty."

He stiffened as his sensitive nose picked up

Midnight's strong feline scent. Sure enough, the large Siamese was padding down the staircase with sure, arrogant steps. Kayla was just behind him. Her colorful shawl was draped over the shoulders of her dress. But Wishbone's eyes were glued to something else—the jingly ball Kayla held lightly in her hands.

"Care to place that in the custody of a reliable canine for the evening?" the terrier offered.

Kayla angled a glance at him that was filled with amusement. "It looks as if your fan club is back for more fun and games, Midnight," she said.

She bent down and held the ball out to Midnight. His teeth closed around one of the rubber bumps. As he took it, the ball let out a melodic jingling that made Wishbone's mouth water. He jumped closer, but stopped when he heard Joe's warning voice speak up behind him.

"We're not here to play, Wishbone," Joe said. "You have to behave tonight, remember?" Taking a few steps toward Kayla, he added, "I promise Wishbone won't cause any trouble."

"What a shame. I was starting to like the little games your canine friends were playing," Kayla said. "I guess we'll have to find other ways to amuse ourselves this evening."

"Um, I guess," Joe said. He put his hands in his pockets and gazed uncertainly at Kayla. "You'll be talking about your trip, right?"

Before Kayla could answer, Mrs. St. Clair came over and took her arm. "Kayla, you must meet the Windoms," said Isabel's mom. "They want to hear all about your trek through the Himalayas."

Mrs. St. Clair led Kayla and the Windoms down the hall toward the living room. Wishbone heard the spine-tingling jingle of Midnight's ball as the cat followed. Wishbone was about to follow himself when the doorbell rang a second time.

"Dinky!" The terrier barked a warm greeting as Dinky trotted into the foyer at the feet of Jimmy and his parents. "Tonight's our chance to get Midnight's ball—after Tracking Dog makes security rounds, that is. Come with me!"

Wishbone heard the quick patter of Dinky's tiny steps as they trotted down the hall. The terrier's eyes and ears took in every detail. He wagged his tail when he saw David and Joe standing in the hallway outside the library. The library door was closed, but Wishbone knew Sam was standing at her post, right next to the closet door.

"Yup! The security team is in place," he barked to Dinky. He trotted through the arched doorway into the living room, then stopped and sniffed the air. "And so is the buffet table!"

The mouth-watering scents of seafood pastry, tender cold cuts, and puffed cheese balls made Wishbone's stomach grumble. Tongue lolling, he took a quick inventory of the activity in the room. Kayla and Isabel's mother were still talking to the Windoms. The housekeeper, Mrs. Hazlett, was adjusting a screen and slide projector at the far end of the room. Wishbone saw Isabel and her father greet a new group of guests.

"Things are picking up, Dinky." Tail wagging, Wishbone wove around the feet of the new guests and headed for the buffet table. "Tracking Dog needs a central command post. A place where I can keep an eye on everything that goes on." He rose up on his hind paws and sniffed at the cheese and crackers. "And make sure the food passes my own personal quality control."

This waiting is driving me crazy! thought Sam.

She leaned against the back of an overstuffed leather armchair in the library and checked her watch. "Seven o'clock," she murmured.

The party had been going for an hour. Sam had heard a steady stream of guests pass by the library door. Yet no one had tried to enter the library. Kayla still hadn't made her move.

"I know she's going to strike," Sam said under her breath. "I just wish I knew when."

The sounds of chattering voices and clinking glasses floated toward her from the direction of the living room. Suddenly, Sam felt that she had to do something—anything.

Three quick strides took her to the hallway door. Pulling it open, she glanced left and right. Joe and David were right were they were supposed to be, on either side of the library door.

"Everything okay?" she whispered.

"So far, so good," Joe answered.

"No one's come out of the living room except to go to the bathroom," David added. He stopped talking as the sound of a fork clinking loudly against a glass sounded from the living room.

"I'd like everyone's attention please," Isabel's father spoke up.

As the noise quieted down, Sam heard him say, "I'm sure you're all eager to hear about Kayla's trip. . . ."

Sam checked her watch for what felt like the zillionth time. Five after seven. "I didn't realize waiting for something to happen would be so hard," she whispered.

"It gets kind of boring just standing here," Joe agreed. "But what else can we do?"

Sam heard clapping as Mr. St. Clair finished Kayla's introduction. "I'd better get back to my post," she whispered. With a quick wave to Joe and David, she shut the door again.

Even through the closed door, Kayla's voice commanded attention. Sam strained to hear what she was saying.

"Thank you for giving me such a warm welcome to Oakdale," Kayla began. "And for hearing about my adventures in India and Nepal." Sam heard Kayla let out a quick laugh before she added, "I guess you could call it the latest installment in the game of my life."

Is that really all life is to Kayla? Sam wondered, as she went to stand next to the closet. *A game*?

She frowned, staring at the solid wooden closet door. "Stealing isn't a game," she murmured. "Soon Kayla's going to find out—"

Sam broke off as the lights flickered and went out. The library was plunged into total darkness!

Chapter Fifteen

When the lights went off, Wishbone had just finished lapping up a morsel of roast beef that had fallen from the buffet table.

"Hey! What's going on?" Kayla's voice cut through the thick blanket of darkness. Other cries rang through the living room. Wishbone could smell the confusion and fear. Gazing into the blackness, he felt the fur along his spine push up.

"Time for Tracking Dog to join the stakeout." Wishbone kept his eyes, ears, and nose on red alert. Making his way through the confused jumble of people, he headed toward the hallway.

"Keep calm, everyone," he heard Isabel's father speak up from the living room. "I'll check the circuit-breakers. We'll have the lights back on in no time."

Wishbone heard the solid footsteps of Isabel's father as he passed by. Then, a moment later, there was a slight rush of air as someone else moved past him in the darkness.

"Hey! Who's there?" the terrier barked out.

No one answered. Wishbone's extra-sensitive canine ears picked up the sounds of a person's footsteps in the hallway. He stiffened from nose to tail. "Joe! David! Someone's coming!"

Then he realized the footsteps were moving away from the library. "Oops! False alarm."

Apparently, Joe had heard the person, too. Above the buzz of voices that echoed from the living room, Wishbone heard his best buddy call softly, "David, did you hear that?" The sound of the voice told the terrier Joe was at his post outside the library door.

Wishbone trotted toward the voice, his nose in the air. "And there's David's scent, too."

"I didn't hear anything," David's whisper came from farther down the hall. "But I don't like this."

"Never fear, guys. Tracking Dog is here for backup and—" Wishbone stopped in his tracks when he heard a new sound—a faint, melodic jingling that made his tail wag.

"Midnight's ball!" Wishbone sniffed the air, jumping from paw to paw. He caught a strong feline scent right behind him in the living room. Midnight!

The jingling sound moved past Wishbone—out of the living room and down the hall. Midnight was taking his treasure in the same direction as the person Wishbone had just heard—away from where Joe and David were stationed.

"That cat is on his own this time. Without Kayla he's no match for Tracking Dog." Wishbone kicked up his heels and trotted quickly toward the irresistible jingling. "Now's my chance!"

Sam's heart was pounding a mile a minute. How long had the lights been out? Two minutes? Three? It seemed like forever.

She leaned firmly against the closet door and stared into the darkness. No one had come into the library. Yet everything inside of Sam told her this blackout was no accident. It had to be a ploy by Kayla to distract everyone so she could steal the diamond necklace and bracelet.

"Go ahead and make your move," Sam murmured.

She didn't let herself be distracted by the cries that rang out from the direction of the living room. Footsteps echoed through the halls. Wishbone and Dinky's barking sounded out from somewhere in the distance, and—

"Finally!" Sam blinked into the blinding glare as the lights came back on again. She turned quickly, trying the door to the closet yet again.

"Still locked," she said, breathing a sigh of relief. She gave a nervous jump as the door from the hallway pushed open. "Oh! It's you, Mr. St. Clair."

Isabel's father stepped into the library, his face tight. "Everything all right in here?" he asked. Joe, David, and Isabel were right behind him.

"No one came in," Sam told them.

The worry lines on Mr. St. Clair's forehead softened just a little. "Thank goodness," he said. "I was sure the thief was going to strike, especially after Mrs. Hazlett told me what happened."

"What?" Sam felt her whole body go tight. "What happened?"

"Someone made an addition to Mrs. Hazlett's list of preparations for the party," Isabel said. She held up a sheet of paper for Sam, Joe, and David to see. "Check out the last thing on the list."

Sam's eyes flew to the bottom of the sheet. Most of the instructions were written in a flowery script. But a final notation at the end had been made in a square, bold print:

WE'RE PLANNING SOMETHING SPECIAL.
AT EXACTLY 7:10,
PLEASE TURN OFF ALL THE LIGHTS.
IT'S A SURPRISE. PLEASE DON'T TELL ANYONE!

"The thief must have written that! So the blackout was a ploy." Sam frowned, turning back toward the closet door "But nothing happened. No one even tried to come in here. The door is still locked."

"The alarm didn't go off, either," David added.

Sam felt as if someone had just stuffed cotton inside her head. Try as she might, she just couldn't make sense of what had happened.

"I don't get it," she said. "I mean, why would the thief go to the trouble of setting up a diversion—and then not even try to take the jewelry?"

She shook her head, as if that would help clear it so she could understand. But all she felt was confused.

"I'm not complaining," said Mr. St. Clair. He reached into his pants pocket and pulled out the key. "But I want to check the safe anyway—just to make sure everything's all right."

"It can't hurt," said Joe. "After all, locks and alarms

didn't stop the thief from stealing Miss Gilmore's ring or the Celtic bracelet at Oakdale Attic Antiques."

Sam shook her head automatically. "Not this time," she said firmly. "I've been right here the whole time. There's no way the thief could have gotten to the safe or . . ."

Her voice trailed off as Isabel's father pulled open the closet door. The safe was wide open. The space where the diamond necklace and bracelet had been was empty!

"I don't believe this," Sam murmured. She felt her stomach twist into a tight knot. "She did it again."

Chapter Sixteen

"She?" Isabel's father echoed. "You think the thief is a woman?"

Sam hadn't meant to tell the St. Clairs about her suspicions until they'd caught Kayla red-handed. But somehow Kayla had slipped through their fingers—again. It was so frustrating!

No more tricks, thought Sam. It was time to be honest with Isabel's family.

"I think Kayla is the thief," she said.

"What!" Isabel cried. "No way!"

Isabel's father frowned, shaking his head. "Kayla would never do something like this to us. We're like family to her," he said.

Sam didn't fully understand it herself. But that didn't make her any less sure that Kayla was the thief they were after. "I know it must sound crazy to you," she said, "but—"

"Look! There's a computer cable," David cut in.

He pointed to the door of the safe. Sure enough, Sam saw that a cable had been attached to the computerized alarm David had set up.

"That definitely wasn't there when we locked the door," Joe said.

Sam jumped toward the closet. As she bent down, she felt her frustration turn to fresh determination. *You haven't outsmarted us yet, Kayla!* she thought.

She followed the trail of the cable with her eyes. It wound behind the squat, metal safe to the rear of the closet. Crouching down on her hands and knees, Sam pushed aside a piece of baseboard that had come loose from the wall.

"There's a hole!" she cried. "The wire goes to the other side."

Sam peered through the opening. It was about six inches square—just large enough for her to see through. "It looks like another closet," she said. She squinted, following the path of the cable to a sleek, rectangular item propped among the boots and umbrellas. "Whoa," she breathed. "There's a laptop computer in there."

"Someone used that to disable the alarm I set up," David said.

"It had to be Kayla!" Sam said. She sat back on her heels, brushing the dust from her hands. The more she thought about it, the more she felt sure she was right. "That's why she arranged to have the lights go out. So she could leave the room and disable the alarm without anyone knowing she was gone!"

"But that hole is tiny. No one could crawl through it," Isabel said.

Sam turned back to the hole—and frowned.

"You're right," she agreed. She measured the distance from the hole to the safe with her arm. Her fingers grazed against the back of the safe—over a foot away from the opening at the front. "And look. The safe is too far away for someone to reach through from the other closet."

"Another impossible crime," Isabel said. "But I still don't think Kayla did it."

Sam's eyes lingered on the small hole, the computer cable, and the open safe. This was Kayla's work. She was positive of it. But she still had to find a way to prove it.

"I'll call the police," Mr. St. Clair said. "You'd better go tell your mother what happened, Isabel. We should break the news to our guests, too. I'm afraid everyone will have to stay put for the time being. The police may want to question people about what they saw."

As they headed for the hall, Sam leaned close to Joe and David. "There's only one person I'm interested in talking to," she whispered. "Kayla."

Joe nodded, glancing up and down the hallway. "I haven't seen Wishbone in a while," he said. "I wonder where he is."

"Victory!" Wishbone kept his teeth firmly clamped around Midnight's colorful ball. As he jumped up and around in his best flip, the jingling bell was music to his ears. "It's ours at last, Dinky! Boy, was it worth the wait!"

Wishbone shook the ball in his teeth, just to hear

the irresistible jingle again. The feel of the satiny reds and blues against his muzzle . . . the splendid squeak of those rubber bumps against his teeth . . . the captivating way lights flashed off the sparkly mirrors . . . it was even more satisfying than he had dreamed a ball could be.

"Here, Dinky. You try it out!"

As the Chihuahua rolled the ball down the hall with a tiny paw, Wishbone turned to look behind them. Midnight sat on the hall carpet some six feet behind them. He drew himself up to his full feline height.

"Don't worry. We'll be happy to give it back . . . after we canines have played with it, that is." Wishbone let out another bark, then trotted down the hall after Dinky. "Yes! Thanks to my expert tracking maneuvers, we did it!"

Wishbone had followed the jingly sound to this back hallway while the lights were out. He'd lost the trail just once—when the jingly bell had fallen silent for a few moments. But his canine patience had paid off. Just moments before the lights winked back on, he'd heard the bell again. And when at last he and Dinky could see . . .

"There it was!" Wishbone let out a happy bark as he recalled seeing the colorful ball come rolling from behind one of the doors along the hallway. No doubt Midnight had been trying to hide from him and Dinky. But Wishbone had leaped forward and gotten his teeth around the ball before Midnight could make away with it.

"You want to play tug of war?" Wishbone clamped

one side of the ball in his mouth. Dinky closed his mouth around a rubber bump on the other side. They pulled the ball playfully back and forth as they made their way past the kitchen and down the front hallway toward the living room. "I'm game, Dinky. Come on!"

Sam watched carefully from the living room doorway while Isabel and her mother broke the news of the stolen diamond necklace and bracelet to the guests. Exclamations of shock and surprise sounded from the guests. But Sam's eyes were fixed on one person in particular.

"Stolen?" Kayla gasped. She turned to Isabel's mother with green eyes that were wide with horror. "How awful!"

She certainly acted as surprised as everyone else, thought Sam. But that was exactly what it was—an act. Kayla was guilty. Proof of it had to be there somewhere.

And I'm going to find it! Sam pressed her lips together in a determined line, watching and listening. She wasn't going to miss a single detail of what went on.

"I just spoke to the police," said Isabel's father, striding into the living room. "They'll be here soon. They've asked that everyone stay here, so they can question us."

"Of course," Kayla said, giving Mrs. St. Clair an understanding smile. "I'm sure everyone will be happy to cooperate. I'll be glad to . . ."

Kayla's voice trailed off. Sam saw concern flit briefly across the young woman's face as she glanced toward the doorway. "Um, I'll be glad to help in any way I can, naturally," Kayla finished.

Why does she look nervous all of a sudden? Sam wondered.

She leaned forward, even more alert. Following Kayla's gaze, Sam spotted Wishbone and Dinky. The dogs had just trotted into the living room. Wishbone had Midnight's ball in his muzzle. Dinky kept jumping playfully at the ball, his tail wagging. As the Chihuahua pulled at the ball with his teeth, Sam noticed the slightest frown wrinkle Kayla's forehead.

Hmm, thought Sam. Kayla was usually so playful herself. Why would she be worried?

Then her eyes fell on the ball. The way Wishbone waved it in his teeth reminded her of something. . . .

Raffles! That was it. Raffles, swinging Lord Belville's hollowed-out Indian clubs in "To Catch a Thief."

Sam's thoughts were moving at the speed of light. She flashed on the jewels that Raffles had found inside one of the clubs, and then on Kayla's worried expression as she watched Midnight's ball.

"That's it!" she said, snapping her fingers.

Joe and David both looked at her as if she were talking gibberish. "What's it?" Joe asked.

"The necklace and bracelet," she said under her breath. "I know where they are!"

She didn't even hear the boys' reactions. Her attention was on Kayla, who was already moving toward Wishbone. But Sam was closer. She bent down and reached for Midnight's ball—then stopped with her hand in midair.

Wishbone's teeth had caught on something. Sam heard the metallic boing of a spring-loaded mechanism. Suddenly, a mirrored section of the ball slid to the side, revealing an opening.

"Look!" Joe said, leaning in behind Sam.

Sam pulled the ball free of Wishbone's teeth and tilted it to the side. A waterfall of diamonds spilled from the opening.

"My necklace and bracelet!" Isabel's mother exclaimed.

Three small cloth-wrapped packages fell out on top of the diamonds. Sam quickly unwrapped them. Moments later, the Celtic bracelet, ruby ring, and gold medallion lay sparkling in her palm.

Chapter Seventeen

Sam gazed in awe at the gems. They sent thousands of shimmering lights sparkling into to the room. But she felt as if nothing could be brighter than the feeling of triumph that welled up inside of her.

"I'd say we've found our thief," she said.

She opened her mouth to say Kayla's name. But as she held up the stolen jewelry, a movement in the doorway caught her eye. It was Midnight. The Siamese cat sauntered into the living room. He walked calmly over to Kayla, twining his sleek body around her legs.

"It was the cat!" Sam realized. "Midnight stole all these things!"

"You can't be serious," said Isabel's father. "Are you trying to say the cat burglar is an actual cat?"

Sam heard the doubtful murmurs that buzzed through the room. She could hardly believe it herself. But when she looked at Kayla, she knew she was right. Kayla smiled at Sam and lifted her glass in a toast. "It appears I've met my match," she said. "Bravo, Sam."

"This can't be. . . ." Mrs. St. Clair's confused eyes jumped from Kayla to the jewelry in Sam's hand. "How could Midnight steal anything?"

"Kayla trained him," Sam said. All of a sudden, the whole thing seemed clear to her. "She told us herself that she's good with animals. She even trained cobras in India. We've all seen how obedient Midnight is. Kayla must have trained him to steal, and to put the stolen loot inside that ball."

There was a look of shock on Joe's face as he leaned against the wall next to her. He gazed down at Midnight for a long moment. "It makes sense," he said. "We couldn't figure out how a person could fit in between the security bars at the *Chronicle* and at Oakdale Attic Antiques. But a cat could. Midnight could have squeezed through the hole in the library closet, too."

"And he could have climbed the tree outside the Kidds' bedroom window, " Sam added. "The branch near the window was too thin to hold a person's weight. But a cat could easily have jumped from it to the bedroom window."

"Wait a minute," David said, shaking his head. "What about the computer? You can't tell me a cat disabled that alarm."

Even as he asked the question, Sam was positive she knew the answer. "That was the one time Midnight had some help. After the lights went out, Kayla snuck around to the back closet and used the computer to disable the alarm," she explained. She spun back around to face Kayla. "Right?"

Kayla raised her glass in a second toast. "Right again," she said. "I planted the computer ahead of time, after I heard Mr. and Mrs. St. Clair talking about their plan."

Isabel's mother turned to Kayla in surprise. "But how?"

"Sound travels marvelously through the heating vents in this house," Kayla said. She reached down to pet Midnight as the cat twined himself around her legs. "I couldn't have pulled it off without Midnight, though."

"Now I know why you had alibis for the thefts, Kayla. Even though you were the mastermind, Midnight was doing the actual stealing." Sam shook her head, crossing her arms over her chest. "When you called Midnight your partner, I didn't realize you meant he was actually your partner in crime."

She would have expected Kayla to look nervous—or at least embarrassed. But Kayla actually seemed proud of what she had done.

"I got the idea for training him while I was working with the cobras in India," Kayla explained. "I was able to teach him to retrieve, and to recognize pieces of the highest quality. Believe it or not, I got the idea from—"

"Raffles," Sam supplied. "You decided to try the same kinds of daring heists A. J. Raffles pulled off in *The Amateur Cracksman.*"

"You're batting a thousand, Sam." Kayla continued stroking Midnight, a smile on her face. "Midnight and I make just as good a team as

Bunny and Raffles, don't you think?"

Hearing Kayla's smug, arrogant tone, Sam felt an angry heat rise to her face. Sam had thought Kayla's love of adventure was alluring. But now she saw it in a different light. "People got hurt, Kayla," Sam pointed out.

"Like me," a boy's voice spoke up.

Sam turned to see Damont standing next to the buffet table. He must have arrived while she was staking out the library closet, she realized. She'd been so focused on Kayla that she hadn't even known he was in the room.

"You set me up, Kayla," Damont said, glowering at her. "You cut letters out of the *Star Reporter* to paste up that note to Sam. And then you planted the newspaper in my pack so I'd get in trouble."

Kayla sent him an amused glance. "Who set up whom, Damont?" she asked. When he didn't answer right away, she gave a wave of her hand that seemed to dismiss him. "I'd hardly call you an innocent victim."

Sam couldn't believe what she was hearing. Sure, Damont had tried to sneak a picture of Kayla. But that was nothing compared to what Kayla had done.

"Maybe it seems cool to live by your wits and play a game that's so exciting and dangerous," Sam said, turning back to Kayla. "But you stole valuable jewelry, things that have been in people's families for generations."

"It's more than that," Isabel spoke up from next to her mother. She frowned, tugging at the ends of her black hair. "You're our friend, Kayla. You've been a guest in our house. Why would you steal from us?"

For the first time, Sam saw Kayla's confident smile falter. "I-I needed the money," she said. "And you have so much. I guess . . . I just didn't think it would matter that much to you."

Seeing the disappointed expressions on the faces of Isabel's family made Sam feel sad, too. She had actually admired Kayla, looked up to her. Now she just felt sorry for her.

"Kayla," Mr. St. Clair began. "I—"

The doorbell interrupted him. Shaking himself, he turned abruptly away from her. "That'll be the police," he said.

He took a step toward the hall, then stopped and faced Kayla once more. "We care about you," he told her. "But it's obvious that you have some tough lessons to learn. And you're going to start right now, by telling everything to the police."

"That pepperoni pizza was top-notch!" Wishbone sniffed at the empty pizza tray on the table in front of him. "Anyone in the mood for seconds?" He cocked his head to the side and gazed at his friends.

It was Monday afternoon. Sam, Joe, David, Ellen, and Wanda had all come to Pepper Pete's to celebrate. After all, it wasn't every day that they caught a thief in Oakdale. Wishbone thought the occasion was worthy of at least two pizzas. But if his friends wanted more, they weren't saying.

"I still can't believe it," Wanda said, fingering the triple strand of colorful beads she wore over her blouse. "What are the chances of a famous heiress like Kayla Cooper being a thief?"

"She had us fooled, too," Joe said, pushing his empty plate into the center of the table. "Until I actually saw the stolen stuff fall out of Midnight's ball, I wasn't convinced she was the person who took it."

Sam shrugged. "She has a special charm, like A. J. Raffles. That keeps people from seeing what she's really up to."

"I'm just glad she was caught and everyone got their jewelry back," Ellen said. She reached forward and plucked a leftover bit of cheese from the pizza tray. "You kids should be proud of yourselves for figuring out the truth."

"Thanks to the dog!" Wishbone barked out. "I'll be happy to accept another slice of pizza as a token of your appreciation."

"Kayla will be paying for her crime, too," David pointed out. "Isabel told me Kayla's going to be doing community service and joining a special rehabilitation program."

"Well, I hope she learns her lesson," Wanda said. "And I can't tell you how grateful I am to you kids that I have my father's ruby ring back—"

She broke off talking as the door to Pepper Pete's opened. Isabel ran in with a newspaper in her hand. "Hi, guys!" Her shoulder bag bounced against her jeans as she hurried over. "Check out the front page. We're famous!"

"That's not the *Star Reporter*, is it?" David asked, eyeing the newspaper doubtfully.

"It's the *Chronicle*," Isabel told him. "The article Sam and I were supposed to write about Kayla was canceled. But . . ."

"I decided to let Isabel do something else instead," Wanda finished with a mysterious smile.

"Really?" Sam said. Wishbone saw the gleam of interest in her blue eyes as she leaned forward. "Check out the front-page photo!" she said. "It's you and me, Wishbone!"

"Where? Where? Where?" Wishbone placed his paws on the edge of the tabletop as Sam spread the newspaper out. There, in the center of the front page, was a grainy photograph of Wishbone and Sam. Sam was holding Midnight's ball, with the mirrored section open and the stolen jewelry sparkling inside.

Wishbone barked at the image and smiled up at his friends. "Didn't I tell you dogs are photogenic?"

Joe squinted at the print on the page. "'Yesterday, the cat burglar who has been mystifying Oakdale residents with her daring and seemingly impossible thefts was finally brought to justice. . . .'" he said, reading the text.

As Wishbone listened, he gazed at the photo of Midnight's ball. The black-and-white image couldn't capture the magical sound of the ball's jingly bell, or the perfect feeling of those rubber bumps in his teeth. And now it was gone.

"'The thief, famous adventuress Kayla Cooper,'" Joe continued to read, "'was caught when fourteen-year-old Samantha Kepler uncovered the stolen jewels inside a toy ball belonging to Miss Cooper's cat.'"

He stopped reading and ruffled Wishbone's fur. "Hey! You're in here, too, Wishbone," he said.

"Yes!" Wishbone gave a joyful bark. "Keep reading, buddy!"

"Listen to this, guys," Joe said. He read on: "'Miss Kepler received unexpected help from a local Jack Russell terrier named Wishbone, who uncovered the stolen jewels while playing with the ball.'"

Wishbone wagged his tail as Sam reached over to scratch him behind the ears. "I couldn't have done it without you, boy," she said.

"Oh! I almost forgot," Isabel spoke up. "I have something for you, Wishbone."

Wishbone wagged his tail expectantly as she reached into her shoulder bag and pulled out . . .

"Midnight's ball!" He barked for joy, taking the ball in his teeth. As the bell's magic jingle rang into the air, Wishbone wanted to leap up in his best flip.

"Kayla forgot to take this when she left," Isabel said. "I figured Wishbone should have it." She reached over to scratch him behind his ears. "You deserve it, boy."

Wishbone jumped down to the ground with the ball in his muzzle. "Thanks, Isabel! I knew this ball was too good for that cat! It looks as if canine justice has prevailed after all." He trotted toward the door, wagging his tail. "I can't wait to show Dinky!"

About E. W. Hornung

Ernest William Hornung was born in 1866 in Yorkshire, England. In his late teens he traveled to Australia to improve his health. The wild Australian bush provided rich material for Hornung, but he didn't emerge as a writer until after his return to England in 1886. In 1893, he married Constance Doyle, the sister of Arthur Conan Doyle, who created the famous detective Sherlock Holmes.

Many of Hornung's early stories were published in magazines. Still, Hornung remained a little-known writer until 1898, when he introduced a new character—A. J. Raffles—society gentleman, talented cricket player, and brilliant thief.

The Raffles stories first appeared as a continuing series in *Cassell's Magazine*. Raffles and his sidekick, Bunny, proved so popular that the stories were later collected as *The Amateur Cracksman* (1899) and *The Black Mask* (1901), and were even adapted to the stage.

During World War I, Hornung helped take a mobile library to British troops fighting in France. He wrote about the experience in *Notes of a Camp-Follower on the Western Front.*

E.W. Hornung died in 1921. But the characters he created has continued to fascinate readers through the years.

Wishbone here. If you like the way I work out a mystery, you'll love my adventures in the classic story of King Midas.

It was Feast City for me the day Wanda spilled her groceries all over the driveway. My boy Joe was pretty happy, too. Wanda's accident gave him a great idea for his own business—Joe's Grocery Delivery. I liked the food angle, but Joe was more interested in profits.

Joe? Hellllooo! Money doesn't buy happiness!

Some guys have to learn the hard way, though. Take King Midas, for example. When he was offered one wish, he chose to turn everything he touched into gold. Great idea? Try eating gold ginger snaps!

Here's a sneak preview....

Now Available

Curse of Gold . . .

Wishbone closed his eyes and imagined himself as Midas. He pictured a palace filled with marble columns. Rose bushes and olive trees filled the courtyards. The palace was in the city of Gordion, the capital of the kingdom of Phrygia.

King Midas sat in a room that faced an open courtyard. The king's chair was made of carved wood with a woven leather seat and soft silk cushions.

Warm breezes from the Aegean Sea wafted through the palace courtyard. The breeze ruffled the fur on the king's back. Midas gnawed on a lamb bone left over from lunch.

Ah, the taste of lamb in my mouth. The scent of roses in my nose! Midas thought happily. He heard the laughter of his young daughter, Ariel, coming from outside.

His tail wagged. Life was good.

Midas stopped chewing and sniffed the air. He sensed someone was approaching.

A servant dressed in a simple robe entered the chamber. His eyes were wide.

"Yes, what is it?" Midas asked. This had better be important, he thought. I hate being interrupted in the middle of a good chew.

The servant bowed to the king. "Your Highness, you have a visitor." Midas could smell the man's excitement and nervousness.

"Who is it?" Midas asked. "You're acting as if the gods themselves have come to call."

The servant nodded. "They have! I mean, one of them has, Your Highness. It is Pan who wishes to see you."

Midas shook his ears. Had he heard correctly? "Pan?" he repeated. He jumped onto all four paws. "You mean, the god Pan? Pan, the god of woods and shepherds?"

The servant nodded again.

Now the king, too, was trembling with excitement from his nose to the tip of his tail. *Just think, a genuine god here to see me! Nothing like this has ever happened to me before!* He quickly shoved his lamb bone under a cushion. "Well, what are you

What does Midas mean when he talks about Pan being "the god of woods and shepherds"? The ancient Greeks believed every place, person, thing, or occupation had a god attached to it. That god had a special connection to the person or place and often helped people who were connected to it.

waiting for? Show him in!"

Midas hopped down from his chair. He began running in excited circles on the floor.

The servant hurried away. A few moments later, Pan entered the chamber. Midas stared at him in awe. The god was twice the size of an ordinary mortal. From the waist up, he looked like a man. But he had hairy legs and hooves like a goat. A wreath of olive leaves crowned the god's shoulder-length, dark curls. He held a bunch of wild berries in one hand. Tucked under his other arm was a wooden flute.

Midas bowed his head all the way down to his front paws. "Welcome to Phrygia, O immortal one."

"Yeah, thanks," Pan answered, yawning. He popped a berry into his mouth. "Charming little kingdom you have here, King . . . uh, King . . ."

"Midas," the king supplied. His tail wagged eagerly. "I am King Midas of Phrygia."

"Oh, right," Pan said with a shrug. "Well, King Midas of Phrygia, I'm here to ask you to do a little job for me."

"Certainly." Midas sat at complete attention. This could be important. Not to mention that Pan might accidentally drop one of those berries onto the floor.

"I need you to help me settle something," Pan explained. He grinned at Midas, his green eyes sparkling. "Somebody has issued me a little challenge."

Midas could hardly believe his ears. "Who would be so foolish as to challenge a god?" he wondered out loud.

Pan burst into laughter. "Good point." He strolled across the floor and sat down in Midas's own chair. The god tucked his enormous goat legs under his body.

Midas waited, his head cocked to one side.

"Anyway, this foolish challenger has suggested a music contest." Pan put his flute to his lips. He piped out a complicated series of notes at dazzling speed. Then he grinned. "I'm sure you know that I play the flute. Shepherd tunes are my specialty."

"Yes, of course," Midas answered.

Pan tucked his flute back under his arm. He tossed a berry in the air and caught it in his mouth. "I met this other fellow in the woods not far from here. He boasted that he was a better musician. So we decided to have a competition to settle the matter. And"—he pointed his flute at the king—"you, Midas, will be the judge."

Midas's chest swelled with pride. "I would be most honored to judge the contest, O immortal one." He was so excited, he leaped into the air and did a little flip. *By next week, he thought, everyone in the empire will be talking about me . . . King Midas!*